STUNG

David Tayoun

BookLocker
Trenton, Georgia

Print ISBN: 978-1-958877-06-7
E-book ISBN: 979-8-88531-290-5

Published by BookLocker.com, Inc., Trenton, Georgia.

Printed on acid-free paper.

BookLocker.com, Inc.
2022

First Edition

Table of Contents

Chapter 1:
Wreckage

Pulling into the far- right lane on I-95 South, in Philadelphia, DJ took the exit, or as it should be named the entrance to the Walt Whitman Bridge which would take him across the River into New Jersey.

Aggravated by the glare of the setting sun in his eyes and becoming more annoyed with himself for leaving the city so late because it resulted in him being caught up in rush hour traffic.

He took the drive into Philadelphia to look at a car he saw for sale, online.

Walking into a car dealership can be like walking into a time sucking machine. "Once they get you sitting down at their desk the conversation can start to resemble one of the many police interrogations I dealt with for no reason," DJ spoke aloud to himself, "First they say you fit the description of a guy waving a gun around and then they barrage you with question after question trying to trip you up. They keep talking and talking until you scream, I DID IT just to get the hell out of there! Or in the case of the car salesperson, okay I give up I'll take it!"

He sat back in his driver's seat and smiled. It was one of those huge gloating, I'm so proud of myself type smiles.

When a cartoonish looking plump, bald salesperson wearing an Easter egg tie greeted him before he had his first foot through the dealership door DJ knew he was in for the duration.

The once in a lifetime, bargain priced car he drove all this way to see, of course had been sold that morning. That's when the high-pressure well- orchestrated sales dance started. Slowly and overly friendly at first with Bob the salesman's determination growing more desperate with each vehicle he presented to his fresh mark.

Bob and the good cop bad cop routine he had going on with his sales manager drove a good bargain, but DJ stood firm using the old "I need to talk with my wife," line.

After three hours of valuable time, he would never, ever get back just like those bogus police interrogations the trio shook hands. DJ promised them he'd call when he and his wife made their decision.

Chuckling and proud of himself for holding his own he merged onto US-42/South, the Atlantic City Expressway. He began daydreaming about times when Deasia and him actually; did make big decisions like buying a car together.

In the rearview mirror he couldn't help but notice a Camaro, rust colored following or more like tailgating him closely. His first instinct was to slam on the brakes and let the jerk hit him but at this rate of speed that could be disastrous.

As the Camaro pulled up beside him, a smaller car directly in front of him slowed down causing DJ to nearly swerve trying to avoid hitting it. When a pick- up truck pulled within inches of his back bumper, he filled with adrenaline.

"What the fuck is going on?" He yelled. "You wanna play?"

Intense fear quickly replaced his anger when he looked to the left again and saw the teenage passenger pointing a gun directly at him.

His need to flee was overpowering but there was nowhere to go. When the shooting started, DJ's mind tried to convince him the nonstop whizzing sounds and bursts of light were familiar. After all his other nickname was pyro.

The sale of illegal fireworks was his successful side gig and had been for many years.

The constant sound of shearing metal however was not familiar, it was terrifying.

Lowering himself as far as he could without obstructing his forward view, he prayed for an opportunity to escape to present itself.

No longer able to feel anything, fearing he was shot and was now paralyzed he knew he had to get away or he would die.

Realizing he was getting close to Atlantic City he looked to his right. He wondered what would happen if he pulled off to the side of the road, floored it and got in front of the smaller car that had him sandwiched in the front.

Taking deep breaths, he realized he had no other choice. He had to make a move, or it was lights out.

With both hands placed firmly on the steering wheel he pressed down on the gas pedal, slowly at first. As he pulled his car onto the grassy area he could hear the twitching and cracking of twigs under the vehicle. The air was still heavy with sulfur and smelled like rotten eggs. It was now or never. He applied more pressure to the gas pedal and within seconds he was side by side with the piece of crap economy car. He floored the Monte Carlo, aggressively.

The element of surprise was on his side, and he was able to catch his breath as he struggled to maintain control and keep his vehicle from sliding further down into a gully. The small car was having trouble catching up with him the dam Camaro was gaining speed and getting close.

DJ turned the steering wheel slightly to the left and kept the gas pedal pressed to the floor. Seconds from being on solid road again well ahead of the Junker he took his eyes from the left and straight in front of him was a garbage heap that included tires. Instinct caused him to veer right to go around the pile. He lost control and sometime between the second and third flip, he passed out.

The aggressors pulled over to get a closer look. Deciding the Monte Carlo was totaled and hoping its driver was too, they high fived each other got back into their vehicles and sped off.

A tractor trailer driver who witnessed the car flipping called 911. He relayed the mile marker to the operator and drove on.

Two Atlantic City police cruisers pulled up to the mile marker at the same time. It didn't take long for them to spot the still smoking wreck. Jeering and racing one another they slid down the steep hill.

It was full on dark now. DJ came to. It took him a minute to remember what happened. He heard voices and thought whoever was shooting at him wanted to finish the job.

Stunned by bright lights that were now shining in his eyes, he tried to get up but couldn't move.

"Don't move!" Someone shouted. He caught a glimpse of a badge. Never in his life was he so happy to see a cop. "Help!" DJ yelled as loud as he could. "We're here to help. Where are you hurt?" That thought hadn't occurred to DJ He reached up to feel his forehead. Once he felt the warm blood it was like a signal to his brain saying yes, I'm hurt and in pain. "My heads bleeding." He started shouting, "I can't move, my legs are stuck!" "More help is here. Breathe normally and we'll get you out of there." One of the cops said.

"But I think I've been shot." DJ yelled.

The two officers looked at each other. One of them radioed the 911 operator and asked if she had the phone number for the trucker that reported the accident. He stepped away from the wreck to make the call. The trucker recalled four cars driving too close to one another and one, the Monte Carlo pulled to the side of the road to avoid hitting the vehicle in front of him. He saw all three cars stop to help, so he didn't bother stopping.

As firefighters worked to rescue him from the wreckage, DJ closed his eyes and struggled to remember every detail of what happened. First he remembered the trash pile. For the life of him he couldn't figure out why these people were trying to kill him.

Convincing himself that the deafening sounds of crunching metal meant that he would be saved any moment, he tried to take a deep breath. The pain in his chest caused him to panic all over again.

He closed his eyes again and remembered how good the beer tasted he had when he made a pit stop to wait out rush hour traffic. "Why'd I stop. If I stayed in traffic this wouldn't have happened."

E.M.S. workers slid him onto a board and placed a brace on his neck. Then they lifted him onto a gurney. In between their barrage of questions as they struggled to carry him up the hill one of the officers fired off his own set of questions.

"Three cars sandwiched me in and started shooting at me. I tried to get away by passing the one on the right, the side of the road and I lost control because of a pile of old tires." "Are you sure you haven't been drinking?" The cop sneered.

"It figures." DJ thought to himself. "Here I am dying and right away this fucker assumes I'm the bad guy. What else is new."

"I stopped at a strip club and had one beer, only one. I've done things in my life that I got away with but this ain't one of them. I'm telling you the truth. These were gang bangers. Yes, they were most definitely shooting at me. Check my car. It's full of bullet holes."

Deciding he was damned if he did and damned if he didn't he made the decision to stop cooperating. These cops didn't even ask him what make of cars the shooters were driving. They assumed he was guilty of something and there was nothing he could do about that now.

A female officer appeared on the scene once they were back up on the side of the road. She asked him if there was someone she could call. Not wanting to scare his mother he asked her to reach in his pocket and get his phone. He told her his wife was listed in his contacts under my baby girl.

She walked away and he couldn't hear the conversation. He was relieved his wife even answered the phone.

"Your wife will get to the hospital as soon as she can." "Thanks." DJ said reluctantly. He didn't want to give any of them an ounce of consideration. Why would he?

Rolling at high speed while lying down facing the opposite direction felt like an amusement ride and DJ was not a fan.

The female officer was quiet. She was sitting in the ambulance, facing the right direction.

It was the E.M.T.'s who were now firing off questions. "Do you have any known allergies, any underlying health issues, or previous surgeries?" The pain in his head and one of his legs was becoming intense. His chest hurt too. It was difficult to breathe and the more he struggled to catch his breath, the more intense the pain in his chest became.

Done cooperating with them too, he closed his eyes and went back to being mad at himself and playing the what if game.

"Why did I stop at that strip club?" He mumbled. "I got enough trouble with the wife."

That was a fact. DJ Davis had more than troubles with his wife. He was so sorry he ever encouraged her to take the pain medication prescribed to her after a car accident on the Atlantic City Expressway.

"Karma is an evil rotten bitch! Here I am now, the victim of a crash on the same damned highway."

That crash was bad, her car was totaled. She had to have surgery on her ankle. It was so broken they had to use screws and pins to put it back together.

Thinking about how badly it must have hurt her made DJ nauseas.

He wasn't going to lie it was nice having her stuck at home although it did put a lot of pressure on him. He had to be Mom and Dad to their three small kids. He cooked, cleaned, carpooled the kids and nursed Deasia back to health.

She recovered. Unfortunately, she never stopped taking the pain medication. When her doctors finally cut her off she was frantic. Seeking out another doctor and then another to accommodate her habit didn't take effort at first.

People had been following him for some time and now they were shooting at him. Did his wife owe them money for drugs? What else could it be?

~

Frantically, Deasia Davis called her neighbor. The elderly woman loved looking after their kids, when needed.

She pulled on an Eagles sweatshirt and brushed her long black hair. After pulling it into a high ponytail she smeared on lipstick. Rushing towards the front door she rattled off instructions to each of the three kids and to Sophie, their neighbor.

Unable to help herself she smiled at the thought of having prescriptions for pain medication readily available, again.

The thought made her feel bad. With everything that happened and as angry as she was with her husband, deep down she couldn't help thinking of the kind, skinny kid that looked like Chris Rock. They met in high school. She wasn't head over heels in love with him anymore, but she did love him.

As she pulled into the AtlantiCare Hospital emergency room parking lot she was filled with fear. She pushed the button to shut her car off and wondered in what condition she would find her husband.

Pushing the lock button on the key fob, she hesitantly walked towards the entrance to the emergency room.

~

In the trauma bay DJ panicked as nurses scrambled to insert an IV and assess his injuries. They were eerily quiet.

"Everything hurts." He mumbled. One of the nurses patted his wrist and assured him they would give him something for pain as soon as they could.

A doctor that looked like he was barely eighteen walked in and listened as the nurses and interns rattled off blood pressure and oxygen readings. Then they got serious. The words head injury, possible punctured lung, broken ribs, and broken leg hung in the air because DJ refused to let them in.

The doctor ordered more bloodwork specifying a drug and alcohol screen and a CT scan, stat.

"More assumptions." DJ thought. His anger resumed.

As attendants lifted him onto the CT scanner a woman entered the room and told DJ his wife was in the waiting room. At first he was relieved. The relief quickly dissolved into indifference.

As the motorized platform he was lying on moved slowly into the machine, DJ felt dizzy before passing out again.

When he came to he was back in the trauma bay. Another doctor, this time a young woman was explaining their findings to him.

"You have two cracked ribs. They'll heal on their own. your right leg has a clean break so it should heal easily. There's a deep gash in your forehead that needs stitching. Your lungs are bruised but the good news is they haven't collapsed and should heal fine. Our worry is your head injury. We're going to admit you and keep an eye on that as well as the other injuries. Overall, Mr. Davis you are one extremely lucky man."

Relieved to hear he was going to live and didn't even need surgery; he took two deep breaths. It hurt!

"How long will he need to be in the hospital?" Deasia asked. The sound of concern in her voice calmed him. "That depends." The doctor answered.

A team entered the trauma bay to staple the cut on his head. Finally, they finally administered pain medication through his IV which relaxed him, while they placed the staples.

Unable to handle seeing the procedure, Deasia went off in search of coffee.

She returned and asked her husband what caused the accident. When she seemed unfazed by his explanation he demanded to know what she knew about the shooting. "Why would you think I knew anything about that?" She snipped.

DJ made the decision not to respond. Instead, he fumed as she sat on a stool in the corner with her head down, texting.

When transport arrived to take him to have his leg set and put in a brace, he told her to go home and take care of the kids.

She told him she'd be back after she dropped the kids off at school.

He wanted to scream, "Don't bother," But instead he bit his tongue.

The disgust between the two of them was palpable.

Thinking of the wreckage that was once his beloved car in that gully hurt but the thought of pulling the plug on the wreckage that was once a happy marriage was unbearable.

Early the next morning DJ woke up to two of Atlantic City's finest sitting in chairs, drinking coffee in his hospital room.

"There were no bullet holes in your car. Do you want to change your story?" Not believing they even looked at his car and convinced even if they did look it over it wasn't done thoroughly DJ said, "None of it was a story. I explained what happened and every word was the truth. I was surrounded and they shot at me. I had no choice but to drive off the road."

"We had the ER physician run a tox screen." Another scare tactic. "And?" DJ knew they found nothing. One beer was all he had. He closed his eyes and his mouth. A few minutes later they told him he could pick up the police report in a few days.

Chapter 2:
The Cop

With each step Jimmy took the keys attached to the belt loop of his brown Carhartt work pants, jingled forward, and rattled back. To keep the rhythm, he kept a steady pace. He worked longer than intended, and he knew Maria would have dinner waiting.

When he retired from the police force due to injuries sustained in an accident during a high- speed chase he promised his wife he would be home for dinner every night, on time. She was eventually okay with him buying a small warehouse to build custom kitchen cabinets only if he promised it would be part-time, a hobby more than a job. Business was slow at first but lately it was increasing steadily.

Jimmy was considering adding custom granite countertops to his inventory. It would mean more money, and more work. He liked the idea of being able to hire a few more people.

Making a right turn from Raleigh Avenue onto Ventnor Avenue it was clear how ethnically diverse Atlantic City continued to be.

With either the Atlantic Ocean, one of many inlets and the bay within walking distance, the medium sized New Jersey city was a great place to grow up. Whether it's still a good place to start a family depends on which of the forty-eight blocks you live on, and of course your tax bracket.

On the left- hand side of Ventnor Avenue is a row of ten, fifteen-year-old, four level townhouses. Each one with identical bluish gray siding and blue, white, and gray striped awnings over the front porches. These homes were the city's answer to much needed lower cost housing for restaurant, casino, and retail workers. On the right side, set back from the street is a mustard-colored arts and craft bungalow built in the 1940's. Next is three sets of brick duplexes that were built in the 1960's. Further down the block on the left is fourteen rowhomes with another fourteen on the right side of the street. When built in the early 1900's to house workers from the Hotel Windsor; the Traymore, and a handful of other new large hotels, they were all identical. Today each home sports its own personality. Over the last century some owners have enclosed their front porches, added additions on the back, some added aluminum siding and others used cedar shingles. Some are well loved and cared for while others are in various stages of disrepair.

Jimmy couldn't miss Benito across the street on the corner rocking, almost jumping back and forth incessantly repeating "This is Jimmy's block don't make me call him, this is Jimmy's block don't make me call him."

During the early 20th century Prohibition laws were ignored in Atlantic City. This left the city booming financially, while other cities across the Country were suffering the effects of the depression. At the same time all types of organized criminals set up shop and planted deep roots, some still operating throughout the dark underbelly of the Jersey Shore today.

It was a constant battle keeping the darkness off this block and a war keeping it out of the city.

Jimmy crossed the street. Benny spotted him and yelled, "Jimmy's here, Jimmy's here." The two shook hands and Benny went back to rocking back and forth this time chanting, "Ezee's home, Ezee's home, Ezee's home."

The front screen door sprung open on the last house in the row and Ezekiel, Benny's much older brother bounced down the porch steps.

"Ezee, what's happening?" Jimmy asked. "Not much Jimmy. It's been a long, windy winter and I'm looking forward to Spring." "Same here Ezee. How's your mom, is she doing okay?" "Winter is always tough on her Jimmy as you know. She can't get out. She's looking forward to the warmer weather too."

Salvador Forero moved young wife and baby boy, Ezekiel to the United States from Puerto Rico in the early 1970's to work in the casinos. Once settled they added a little girl they named Luisa. Sal worked fulltime in the maintenance department of one casino after another, moving another rung up the ladder which each job move. Wanting to provide the best for his family, he took on freelance repair person and construction jobs on the side. Once Ezee was old enough he worked construction alongside his father.

Later in life with a twenty-four-year-old son and a twenty-year-old daughter Sal and Fausta welcomed Benito into their family. It was obvious baby Benny was different within months of his birth. The diagnosis of autism came years later.

Fausta never recovered from nerve damage suffered during the emergency C-section to deliver Benny, and she was confined to a wheelchair. With a disabled wife, a special needs son, and a daughter in college Sal and Ezee worked day and night to cover the family's astronomical bills.

Sal suffered a massive heart attack eight years earlier while on a construction site and passed in the hospital a few days later. Luisa graduated college and moved to Puerto Rico with her husband to open a health clinic. This left Ezekiel to care for his mom and younger brother. Ezee's wife refused to move in with his mother and his mother refused to move in with Ezee and his wife.

This left Ezee in a constant state of guilt because he was working to keep both households afloat while also trying to be there for everyone who needed him.

Jimmy and Maria did what they could to help. They picked up groceries, made sure Benny remembered to put the trash out and gave the two rides to doctor appointments when possible.

"Hey Jimmy, there's a new dealer hanging on this corner. The bastard put his hands-on Benny, on my little brother, and told him to get off the corner. I'm so pissed Jimmy. Have you seen him? Do you know who he is, who he's working for?"

"Now Benny saying, call Jimmy talk makes more sense, you teach him that? Jimmy asked Ezee. Both men laughed.

"I haven't seen him yet, but I'll be keeping my eyes open." "Appreciate that man," Ezee answered, "I'll try to be around more at night but a friend, my neighbor was in a bad wreck last night. His cars totaled. He's one of those poor guys that can't catch a break. I wouldn't believe it if I didn't witness it every day with my own eyes. It's dramatic man, the poor bastard."

"I have that old jeep if he needs to borrow wheels until he gets back on his feet."

"Thanks Jimmy, I'll pass that on." Ezee said shaking Jimmy's hand.

Fausta wheeled herself to the front door and called her sons inside to eat, in Spanish. "Go home Jimmy," she hollered in English, "Maria has your meal ready." "I'm goin, I'm goin."

Jimmy assured Ezee he'd keep an eye out for Benny and the latest scumbag who was trying to take up residence on *their* corner. He said goodnight and ran across the street.

The Tayborn house at 3814 Ventnor Avenue was a single split level the couple had built on property owned by Maria's grandparents. This year they would celebrate their 30th wedding anniversary and thirty years in their home.

Lance, the couples medium sized mutt greeted Jimmy at the door by jumping in circles on his back two legs and barking excitedly. "I'm home," Jimmy yelled. "I'm putting dinner on the table, come sit," Maria yelled back.

After giving Lance a quick belly rub, he hung his jacket on a wooden coat tree and removed his weapon from the shoulder harness, checked the safety and placed it in the top drawer of a small chest in the foyer. He locked the chest and then hung the empty harness on the coat rack then walked up the five steps into the living room and then into the kitchen.

"You're late," she said trying to sound angry. "I stopped to talk with Benny," He answered while bending to kiss her on the cheek. "How was your day doll," trying to sound more interested in her than he was in the slab of meatloaf he dropped onto his plate.

Maria went on and on about going to the supermarket that afternoon. She dropped groceries off to her mother and to Fausta. His bride was so kind, and he knew he should be paying attention to her but the cop in him wanted to catch the latest drug dealing slimeball in action. He didn't dare mention it to Maria, he didn't want to upset her.

Instead, he formulated a plan.

Lance bounced into the kitchen and sat at Jimmy's feet. "How bout we go for a walk you little pain in the ass," Jimmy said sending Lance dashing down the steps to sit and whine by the front door. They both laughed.

Jimmy put the dishes on the kitchen counter and Maria rinsed them and put them in the dishwasher. "Go take him for his walk and be careful out there, we have a new drug dealer on the corner." "You've seen him?" He asked, surprised. "I noticed him when I closed the front blinds last night." He bent down and kissed her other cheek, "I'll be careful."

"You can't take the Jersey outta my girl," Jimmy thought, "She doesn't miss a thing." He put Lance's leash on and then systematically put on his holster and inserted the weapon. When he reached for his coat Lance could no longer be patient and he started to bark.

The two walked three blocks north, crossed the street and headed south.

Stopping at a house across the street from his own home, Jimmy stopped to pick up a Seven-Eleven Big Gulp cup. He walked up to the side of the house and put it in a trash can. "Slobs." He bought this house a few years back as a rental investment.

He could make out the shape of a man on Benny's corner and several people walking towards the figure.

Chapter 3:
Boomer

This corner is no different than a million other corners across the United States. It starts out with a dealer on the corner and a little bit of foot traffic. Then the cars come and go, some speeding, some blocking the flow of traffic, most blaring music from large speakers.

Neighbors call 911 and if lucky a patrol car will occasionally drive by, chasing the dealer and customers but before the cop gets to the end of the street business is back to normal.

Next comes those derelicts shooting up heroin or smoking meth in between homes and then passing out. Unsuspecting homeowners go out their side door to put garbage in their cans and find a junkie sleeping in their bushes. They call 911 and if a cop shows up he wakes the junkie up and chases them off. In most cases they are back again the next night.

It doesn't take long before cars and homes are broken into, the violence starts, and gunshots become a nightly occurrence.

Elderly residents start to die off or move into senior communities selling their lifelong homes off to flippers or worse yet abandoning them which makes the homes the perfect location for dozens of junkies to crash. One drug house leads to another and then another.

Even if a bunch of neighbors get together and insist the police bust the dealer, the arrest only slows them down a few hours, at most a few days. They'll bail out and get right back to work, leaving homeowners feeling completely frustrated and in many cases terrified.

As he got closer Jimmy tried to identify the guy but there was nothing familiar about him. He was big. Jimmy and Lance crossed the street and walked about fifteen feet past the dealer. Turning abruptly Jimmy walked towards him and stopped a foot from him.

"Man listen, you can't deal here." Jimmy said. "Get off my corner old man," the punk answered. Jimmy stood his ground. "I'm not playing with ya kid you can't do this crap here." The dealer got in Jimmy's face and screamed, "SCRAM BEFORE YOU GET HURT BOOMER." He walked away laughing.

"What did he call me?" Jimmy asked under his breath as he started walking the other way.

Two skinny scraggly looking men walked toward the dealer as the dealer cocked his head back and glared at Jimmy smugly. As Jimmy approached them, Lance growled softly. "Listen guys, I'm retired 5-0, a cop you get that right? I'm out here taking notes and photos of everyone that buys drugs on this corner. Do yourselves and favor and walk on." The two men turned and walked, slowly in the opposite direction. Three other potential customers did the same.

The dealer screamed, "GET OFF MY CORNER!. I ain't gonna tell you again." Jimmy stayed calm but firm. "Kid I'm telling you; I'm retired 5-0 and I'm building a case here. If your smart you'll bolt, NOW!"

The dealer crossed the street, took his cellphone out of his pants pocket, and made a call. He continued to glare at Jimmy.

Continuing to stand his ground Jimmy turned one of the dealer's customers after another away.

Shoving the phone back into in his pocket, the dealer stomped away.

"That's what I thought," Jimmy said to the dog, Let's go home buddy. Lance having sat too long tugged on his leash. "It's a fulltime job keeping this block clean isn't it partner," he said to Lance. "We won the first battle with that clown."

Maria watched the whole scene playout from a small opening in the curtains that lined the large bay window in their living room. She wished her husband would give up his crime fighting obsession but at the same time she also knew if he didn't do it they wouldn't be able to stay here, on this block, their block.

Her mind wandered back to the night of the accident. Every cop's wife imagines the worst at one time or another while at the same time hoping and praying for the best.

That night she'd been out with her mother. They had dinner at a small Italian restaurant in town and talked for a long time over coffee and tiramisu.

Once home Maria sat in the living room. She happened to be looking out the front window as a patrol car pulled up. She assumed Jimmy was taking a break. When the car parked on the street instead of in the driveway, she lost her breath. Frantically she started praying. Lance barked erratically as the knocking on the door started. She couldn't make her legs move. She didn't want to hear whatever the message was to her from the other side of that door.

Her cell phone rang and vibrated off the kitchen counter hitting the floor with a loud thud. She forced herself to walk into the kitchen and pick it up.

"I'm okay doll!" It's Jimmy she kept whispering to herself over and over. She hadn't really heard another word he said. Tears of relief ran down her face. Lance was still barking at the front door. Maria wiped her tears with the palms of her hand and with her legs still shaking and wobbly she made her way down the steps to the front door.

"He's going to be fine," the young officer said over and over as fast as he could. "If you'd like I can take you to the hospital." "Come in." she instructed him.

Maria remembering her husband was on the phone, she put it back to her ear and told Jimmy she'd be there soon. She put her phone and its charger in her purse. Reached for a small gray pitcher she kept on top of the refrigerator she poured out a handful of quarters. She dumped them into her purse and grabbed a heavy sweater from the hall closet.

Paul, the young officer insisted on helping her down the steps and into the front passenger seat of his cruiser. She was finally able to catch her breath and now felt strong enough to know what happened to her husband.

"He was in pursuit of a suspect and was somehow side swiped by another car, we aren't sure yet if it was the suspect's car that hit him. All I know is they are evaluating Jimmy's injuries but he's going to be fine, there's nothing life threatening.

Maria breathed a deep sigh of relief.

The back- parking lot by the ambulance entrance was full of police cars. She wondered if they were all there for Jimmy or if criminals were unusually busy getting hurt. The change of seasons always caused an uptick in criminal activity, and it was the beginning of Spring.

~

"Spring," Maria shook her head. No wonder I'm thinking of that night! This is the same time of year it happened. Four years ago, this week!

~

Paul guided her through the back entrance of the hospital and down a long brightly lit hallway. He pushed open a door that led to a small, private waiting room. Every seat was occupied by an officer.

They all stood as Maria walked in.

A nurse ushered her back down the hall, through two sets of automatic doors. While the nurse opened the sliding door to the bay that held her husband she couldn't help noticing a bronze plaque on the wall. *This trauma bay was donated by Frank Sinatra.* "Casino family." She said under her breath.

Relieved to see him awake and alert she gently put her arms around him and kissed his forehead. His neck was in a brace. "It's my back babe, it hurts!"

A doctor who looked too young walked in with a serious, almost grim look on his face. "You have a concussion, Jim. Best case scenario it heals itself in a week or so. Two of your ribs are cracked. I'm guessing caused by the airbag and you have a couple of compression fractures in your lower back. Then of course there's the whiplash. All these injuries unfortunately tend to be painful and have long recovery times. The good news is you should recover fully. "No surgery?" Jimmy asked. "No. Not now anyway, hopefully that doesn't change." Maria and Jimmy looked at each other and smiled. "We'll keep you for a few days to keep an eye on the head and back injuries, but my guess is you'll be fine."

Jimmy looked at the doctor and said, "Hey, Doc, this is nothing compared to the ass whomping I took so my wife wouldn't lose her job, when we first met." Maria laughed, "That's not how I remember it happening." The doctor shook his head and said, "As curious as I am, I have other patients to see." Steve said, "I have time and I think it's interesting and would love to know how you snagged Maria when so many others tried and failed." Jim started by saying, "Well you know how they wanted us to use control and resistant techniques, in an attempt, to reduce *use of force* lawsuits. So, I guess some jackass politician, after watching a Steven Seagal movie thought that reflected real life. Did he believe that cops with a short five-hour training course could replace years of training from someone that is a professional martial artist, someone like Seagal? So, Maria got a contract, you know probably because of some minority female charity." Maria trying not to laugh, glared at her husband. She knew that he was trying to get a rise out of her. "Just because I was repeating some of my favorite scenes from martial arts movies as a kid with Joe and Pete, she decides to make an example of me. She told me, don't go easy on me swing as hard as you can. Hell, I practically twisted myself in a pretzel and put the cuffs on for her." Steve laughed knowing that the clowning around part was the only truth from Jimmy's story. Maria said, "If you 're done, and only if your done I'll tell my side of this story." Jimmy rolled his eyes and said he would only cut in if she couldn't remember something, or if she was making things up.

The pain medication given by the doctor finally kicked in and Jimmy was doing more mumbling then talking before he passed out. Maria continued, "Yes I remember him making me watch those old Black and white Chinese movies dubbed in accented English to prove that he was using actual techniques after our training session. One was called the Crab Technique, and another was the Drunken Fighter Technique and of course there was the Fighting Monk Technique. Although they were actual techniques, he was far from mastering anything. He finally confessed to being a third-degree brown belt in Tae Kwon Do but last practiced it ten years before joining the police department. Mind you. I had no knowledge of any of this when I saw him hamming it up before my training session. So, I asked him to be my aggressor to show the effectiveness of the Tae Kwon Do counter fighting techniques using your opponent's weight and aggression against them. After his first He-Man attack, I deflected throwing him to the ground. He subconsciously went into his training form, but a third- degree brown belt not fluid in his form is no match for a tenth-degree black belt that hasn't had a break in training for 20 years.

We went at it for a good hour. I avoided him but knocked him down every time the opportunity presented itself. The point was made that a thin female obviously unmatched in size and strength was able to wear down a mean bear, at least until help arrives or eventually the opportunity presented itself to take him out.

We never got to finish the session because time ran out. He insisted on proving that he learned his techniques from these old movies and by the time we were done he offered me dinner and drinks and one thing eventually led to another. I was the loser because this neanderthal got me as the prize." She laughed and kissed his forehead as he slept.

When he returned to work, he was assigned to a special *No Crime* task force. It was more of a desk job. With it came a new partner, Tommy. Jimmy missed Steve, his long- time partner but he did like Tommy, at first.

Seeing the writing on the wall and knowing he wouldn't be able to serve the way he wanted to, Jimmy looked to the future. He and Tommy went into business together. At once Jimmy realized he made a big mistake.

Tommy was a dirty cop, and he didn't even try to hide it. He bragged about having a million dollars in a special account. Money he skimmed, thousands of dollars after confiscating cash from dealers during various drug busts in Atlantic City. Not wanting anything to do with him on the force or in business Jimmy refunded the down payments for renovation work they collected out of his own pocket.

Not happy that Jimmy reneged on their business venture, he tried to set Jimmy up.

When they first started working together, Tommy told him, "If you ever find yourself in a room with some suits, saying they don't want to hurt anyone while shaking your hand and telling you they just want to get to the bottom of it, they are going to screw you, and they are looking to lock you up. Be prepared.

Driving down the street on his way home from work one day, he noticed four men on the roof of a house across the street. He didn't see a work truck out front and after driving around the block there wasn't one out back either. "They don't have a permit."

This was the first time he saw someone at the property in over a year.

He pulled his car over and asked. They yelled back down from the roof, yes they had a permit. Jimmy was sure they didn't. All contractors place something with their business name on it, a truck, or a sign in front of any property they are working on.

An elderly couple owned the property. They passed- away and left it to their daughter who lived in Washington, D.C. Like most other absentee property owners that make up seventy five percent of Atlantic City property ownership, she hired a local real estate company to manage the rental. The real estate companies care more about collecting fees and rent then they do about who they rent property to. Complaints by tenants about the poor property conditions are managed by paying off code officials rather than fixing the problems.

These houses are like cancerous tumors in the neighborhood. They are used by drug users to get high. The police are constantly being called for domestic violence, for fights and because people refused to leave the property once the drugs are all used up.

Unable to miss the workers putting plywood over the existing shingles, and then putting new shingles on top of that plywood, he was sure they had no permit.

Jimmy called code enforcement. As he guessed they had no permit. The code enforcement officer went to the property and issued a stop work order. He also gave them a $2000 a day fine for any day they work, up until they got a permit.

A few days later, frustrated after paying a $2000 fine the homeowner put the house up for sale, as is. At first she wouldn't sell it to Jimmy but three months later she relented because no one was offering even close to what she was asking.

Jimmy was able to get Code Enforcement to Red Tag the building for past unpermitted construction of illegal separate apartment units and it was boarded up and labeled uninhabitable. Jimmy knew he was paying more than what the property was worth, but he thought it was better to pay more now then lose even more with the continued deterioration of his block which would also affect the value of his home.

Soon after he bought the property Jimmy was called to his captains' office. The captain disliked Jimmy because he refused to go along to get along. Once in the office the captain shook Jimmy's hand and introduced him to Frank Furhman and Frank's partner. Both men were FBI agents.

"We're not trying to hurt anyone we just want to get to the bottom of something." The captain said. "Oh fuck." Jimmy thought.

Knowing he did nothing wrong was no comfort to him. He'd seen enough innocent guys that were going after bad cops go down through the years.

Tommy made bogus reports incriminating Jimmy. It took a few weeks, but Frank listened to Jimmy. After a thorough investigation he was able to verify Jimmy's version of the events and was able to clear him.

Although he was cleared of doing anything wrong his injuries were continuing to cause him pain. The stress of the investigation didn't help.

The city doctors told him the MRI of his back showed he reached his maximum medical improvement. He would need to pass a physical endurance test. Jimmy was told he would be notified when the test would be scheduled.

The notification arrived and his test was scheduled for his birthday. Maria made plans for them and a couple of friends to go on a dinner cruise that evening.

Despite trying to reschedule the test for a different day it was set in stone and failure to show up would be an automatic fail. So early that morning Jimmy was more determined than ever to pass the test in record time and have a great celebration that night. He had no doubt he would be back to his old assignment with his old partner Steve in no time.

He was met by a nurse who had lots of forms for Jimmy to sign. Next came a drug test to confirm that he did not take any medication for pain. Jimmy never took what they gave him he didn't like the way it made him feel and he had seen too many people get hooked.

Jimmy tried to make a joke about the test being done on his birthday a thoughtful gift from his employer, but she was all business. Jimmy made it through all the push-ups, the stair climbing, and jumping jacks. Next was lifting or dragging various weights over different obstacles. The last task was the 3-mile run in 20 minutes.

The first mile Jimmy ran at a quick pace. Entering the second mile the pain started shooting across his back, and then down his legs. His feet went numb, and an intense sensation of pins and needles made it increasingly difficult to keep his pace. Halfway through the second mile, not being able to feel his feet Jimmy stumbled and collapsed. He hit the running track with his hands and face scuffing both resulting in minor cuts and bruises.

He was forced to retire.

At his birthday dinner, Jimmy tried to put on a good face on for Maria and their guests but the weight of being forced to retire at the early age of thirty was weighing heavy on him. He was not the kind of guy who wanted to sit on a porch and rock his days away.

Steve came from the bar with two beers and said, "Boy that nurse beat you up as bad as Maria did in the academy. Come on step out onto the deck with me."

It was a great night on back bay with the casinos in the foreground. The water was calm, and the low hum of the boat engines was soothing. Steve said, "Congratulations you lucky bastard." Jim said, "How do you figure that?" Steve said "You just hit the lottery. You got about ten years on and now you are walking with sixty-six and two thirds of your salary. You never have to worry about the corruption in the department and people constantly trying to get you fired. We both know they tried a half a dozen times, even after you still cover up for those scumbags. Jim you're not like me or these other cops you were in law school, you came from a business family." Jim replied, "And, what does that mean." Steve said, "Hell you already have rental property and do side construction work. So, you will find something to do. Not like the rest of us who only wanted to be cops. Hell, we would either drink ourselves to death or do some other drug because we wouldn't be able to think of anything else except get hired as a security guard that sits at a desk by a door. You have a steady salary with the pension so you're not starting from scratch."

A light went off in Jimmy 's head. He realized how true, Steve's comments were, and he realized the opportunity he had in front of him if only he would stop feeling sorry for himself.

Steve said, "Don't be too successful or they'll demand you be retested and forced back to work, so they can fire you. Now let's go in and have some fun since I'm your only friend and this is your birthday slash retirement party."

~

Lance's nails tapped on the tile floor in the foyer. "We're back," Jimmy yelled.

She was relieved. He grabbed the tray full of snacks she prepared from the kitchen counter, and they went downstairs into the family room to watch tv.

"Chased another one," he started, "I should've kicked his ass for what he did to Benny. If he comes back I will." "Oh stop!" Maria scolded.

"Hey, do you know what a boomer is, what does that mean?" "It means you're officially old." She laughed.

Chapter 4:
The Picnic

Ezee wasn't popular per say but he was well known for throwing huge neighborhood parties. His house was directly across the street from the Atlantic City Bay. The large grassy area across the street from his house was perfect for large gatherings.

Neighbors rolled their grills over, set up tables, chairs, music, and it's on. Everyone brought either a platter of food, some sort of dessert, a case of beer or a bottle of liquor.

And then there was DJ, or as he was known in the neighborhood, Pyro. He always supplied the fireworks show and most in the neighborhood appreciated the show, except for one. There's always that one neighbor that must bitch about something and ruin it for everyone. She has the police and fire department on speed dial.

These aren't the "safe" backyard type fireworks. These are the professional grade. DJ bought and sold them illegally.

Although he was always invited, Jimmy never attended one of his friend's famous picnics. As a cop it was always frowned upon to socialize with these characters. As a retired cop these still weren't his people.

Now that he wanted to rent space in the warehouse, Ezee thought it would be a clever idea for Jimmy to show up and meet some people. As a contractor himself he knew a lot of guys in the business.

In his jeans, flannel shirt, and work boots he stood out in the crowd. "It's 52 degrees and April in New Jersey and look at these morons," He whispered under his breath, noticing how many in the crowd, and it was a crowd were wearing tank tops, shorts, and sandals.

Making his way to the food table he handed the three boxes of Tastykakes that he picked up at the 7-Eleven off to a pretty, young woman. Spanish, he thought noticing her brilliantly shiny, and long black hair and dark eyes. The rock on her left hand was at least a full carrot. He quickly scanned the crowd looking for a man that might be eyeballing him for eyeballing her. Not that he was worried.

A slap on his back startled him. "Jimmy, I'm so glad you could make it brother," Ezee said loudly as he grabbed Jimmy's hand for a quick shake. "Let me introduce you to some good peeps." "I can hardly wait," Jimmy thought to himself. Aloud he said, "Sure."

Making their way through the still growing crowd, Ezee gave Jimmy quick bios on the plumber, carpenter, and window guy he introduced him to.

Out of the corner of his eye he couldn't help noticing a stocky, Mexican man cornering the Spanish girl. He had tattoos but from the distance Jimmy couldn't make them out. He felt a twinge of disappointment. He'd hoped she was married to some professional type. A few minutes later a Black man wearing a brace on his left leg walked up behind her. Sliding the hair off her shoulder, he kissed her neck.

There's a whole lot more to that story, Jimmy thought.

He recognized the guy. As a cop he spoke with him after receiving calls, on several occasions about illegal fireworks, right here at this park. The guy had an attitude, a definite chip on his shoulder. Jimmy wasn't a ball buster and always told the guy to knock it off with the fireworks because neighbors were complaining and left it at that.

As Jimmy was fixing himself a plate of barbecue chicken, corn on the cob and potato salad, the man approached him and Ezee. He couldn't help but notice the Black Lives Matter tee shirt the guy was wearing. "One of those." Jimmy mumbled.

"Jim, this is DJ" Jimmy extended his hand. DJ reluctantly took his hand and shook it. "I remember you. You're the cop right?" "Retired cop." Jimmy answered.

"Is that a thing?" DJ continued. "Thought once a cop always a cop. All that loyalty shit and all." "Well, he still has the giant chip on his shoulder." Jimmy thought to himself.

He couldn't see himself becoming friendly with this one anytime soon.

"Actually; that's priests, once a priest, always a priest," Jimmy answered sarcastically. DJ. walked away. Jimmy leaned in and whispered to Ezee, "Well come to think of it my oath doesn't have an expiration date on it." They both laughed. Ezee knowing that it was Jimmy's character to be one of the guys, cop or not. The difference was, he will always do the right thing.

"Excuse DJ's attitude. He's harmless and deep down a decent guy," Ezee stated, "He's got major troubles with the wife, so he's looking for any extra work he can get." "I get that," Jimmy said. "So, you'll still lend him the jeep when he gets that brace off his leg?" "That's the guy?" Jimmy was more than surprised. "Seriously Ezee, that guy?" "How's that chicken?" Ezee asked. "Amazing!" They both laughed. "I know DJ's rough around the edges but trust me he really is a good guy." Ezee stressed the point again. "I'll keep that in mind." Jimmy answered.

~

Desperately needing more pills than what he was giving her the money for, Deasia went by her friend Angela's house. Having DJ laid up at home with pain killer prescriptions was great while it lasted. She knew Ang's brother would have some Oxi for sale. Instead, DJ introduced her to Danny, her new boyfriend.

DJ knew her addiction was getting worse. She was needing an Oxi every few hours to keep up with the house and deal with their kids. Eventually she needed something to get her to sleep, another something to wake up and the Oxi's to get through the day. It got expensive quick.

DJ almost wished she'd start smoking crack; it'd be cheaper. If anyone knew Deasia it was him, and he knew her well enough to know she would never lower herself to sucking on the pipe.

They met in high school. He was instantly attracted to her. She was gorgeous. Even after three kids she was still hot, even hotter.

His wife loved nice things though and he felt good about himself when he was able to provide them for her. He worked his ass off to provide her with a brand- new Infinity X-50 to drive after the accident. For their anniversary he surprised her with the full carrot replacement engagement ring she'd been dreaming of forever.

Even though he worked three jobs, the couple lived far above their means.

Dear Lord, her hair and nail appointments on top of the drugs and bills were killing him. Then there were the kids. Dance lessons, music lessons, sports, and designer clothes. "Kids don't need damn designer anything!" He would tell her, but she insisted. Her kids would never be dressed like paupers. No way!

Cutting her off during the week and only providing her with money for pills on the weekends was supposed to make things better, normal again. Instead, she was miserable and always had somewhere else to be. He was missing work because he had to pick the kids up from school. All three of them took part in sports and his little girl had gymnastics and dance classes. Luckily, his bosses were willing to collaborate with him and accommodate his constantly changing schedule.

Their arguments were getting louder, and he was afraid they were close to getting physical. To avoid any more confrontation, he produced a solution. He told her she could have a few pills each day, but she had to start taking better care of the kids so he could work to pay for her ever- growing list of expensive habits.

She was still wandering while the kids were in school. He assumed she'd been spending time together with girlfriends, even buying extra pills off their husbands or boyfriends.

Before long, Danny was happy to introduce both women to a new, less expensive version of happy, and to supply them with all the heroin they needed to get through their day.

Sticking a needle in her arm was the last thing Deasia ever thought she would do. It didn't take long for her to forget how horrified she was by the idea. Now it was an escape from a powerful need she couldn't explain. It relieved her physical and mental pain, at least for a little while. And it was so much cheaper than the pills. With the money DJ was giving her, she'd be able to use all the heroin she wanted and have some money left over for a pair of shoes now and then.

Dropping her kids off at school and then hanging all day with Magda at her house became her routine. She was aware of all red flags but chose to ignore them. The high was more important.

Danny had guns all over the house and dozens of people were coming and going all day long. In between hits she could feel the tension in the house, or it was her own intense fear. Of course, the negative feelings only lasted until the next time she hit up.

She had heard of MS13 and guessed that's who or what Danny was. He had a lot of enemies and was always looking over his shoulder. A group of thugs surrounded and protected him day and night. They were protecting him out of fear rather than loyalty.

Deasia knew she was better than all of this, but she couldn't or even didn't want to give up the only happy she'd felt in a long time.

Every now and then Danny would give the women money to spend the day at a spa. Magda said he did it because he needed them to be out of the house so he could get business done. Deasia could only imagine what that business was.

~

One afternoon Danny insisted Ang take a ride with him. She told her friend she'd be back in an hour.

Deasia had no idea what she was getting herself into when she accepted a sandwich from Danny's cousin Raffa. They sat, talked, laughed, and ate together at Ang's kitchen table. He looked at her like he couldn't wait to hear what she was going to say next.

It wasn't long before Deasia and Raffa made their way upstairs to a mattress on the floor in a back bedroom. Intense guilt filled her for a moment, but she did her best to push any thoughts of her family from her mind.

Running her hand along a scar on his side, afraid to ask what happened, she asked anyway. "I got shot with a thirty-eight, twice," He said, "Pointing to another scar on his stomach." Her heart sank. "Twice! You're so lucky to be here." She said hugging him.

He went on to tell her he was born in El Salvador and his parents brought him to California when he was eighteen months old. They settled in the suburbs of Los Angeles. His parents still live there with his three younger sisters and younger brother, who were all born in California, in the United States.

"When I was in ninth grade I got involved with Mara Salvatrucha," He started explaining, "and I got in trouble. I continued to get in trouble and when I was nineteen I got deported."

"What is Mara Salvatrucha?" Deasia asked already guessing she knew the answer. "A gang, MS13, you've heard of it, nothing good I'm guessing, but Mara comes from marabunta, which is a fierce type of ant that kills by swarming their enemies in huge numbers. Salvatrucha is a combination of the words Salvadorian and trucha which together means alert. Thirteen comes from the letter M being the thirteenth letter in the alphabet." "But is there anything good I should hear?" She asked softly.

"We're a family," He smiled.

"Where are you from?" He asked. "I was born here in Atlantic City and have lived here my whole life." "What's your nationality?" He asked. "I'm Black, Italian, and Puerto Rican. I don't mind being called those. Just don't call me African because I'm not," she smiled at him and continued, "Honestly I prefer being called Deasia or Dee. Wouldn't the world be a much nicer place if we all simply called each other by our names?"

Things continued to heat up between the two of them to spite constant warnings from Magda.

Deasia simply wasn't thinking clearly, and Magda was terrified there would be violence that would escalate quickly between DJ and Raffa. Her worst fear was that the gang would get involved and she didn't want any of that for her friend or her friend's kids.

~

DJ felt badly thinking it, but he had a lousy feeling his instincts had been right all along about his wife. He felt sick. Out of the corner of his eye he watched as this guy, judging from his tats, was no doubt a gang member and he was acting familiar, too familiar with his wife.

As the two of them seemed to be having a heated conversation, DJ interrupted them. “Hey baby,” he said reaching for Deasia’s hand. “Hey DJ,” She answered nervously, “This is Angie’s man’s cousin Raffa.” DJ held his hand out, “Nice to meet ya man.” Raffa took DJ’s hand, shook it, and without saying a word turned and walked away.

DJ grabbed his wife’s arm and pulled her close, and whispered in her ear, “Whatever it is, or it isn’t it stops now!” With that he pushed her and let go of her arm.

That was the first time he noticed the bruises on the inside of her arm. Her veins looked so dark. He’d seen that before. His cousin was a junkie. Stunned and feeling sick to his stomach he turned and walked away from her.

When DJ looked at her all she could see was how disappointed he was in her. Lately it was so much more than disappointment. Now he was disgusted with her. It hurt deeply. He’s the one who got her into this mess in the first place. He was the one who insisted she take the pain medication. When he blamed it all on her, it made her furious.

That night the couple fought loudly for hours.

He offered to send her to rehab. Promised her that they could get their family back on track. They could be the picture- perfect family they once were again, if only she would check herself in to a facility. “It won’t be for that long baby. The time will fly by, and you’ll be home where you belong.” She flat out refused again and told him there was nothing he could do or say that would change her mind.

When he threatened to take her car, kick her out and keep the kids from her she went crazy. She broke everything in her sight, lamps, dishes, and the kid's toys. When she threw his phone, he tried to catch it. It flew over his head, across the room, shattering a glass shelf and the face of the phone.

It ended with her locking herself in their bedroom.

He left and ended up sleeping on Ezee's couch.

As soon as she heard the front door close, she called the police. When they saw the condition of the house they put out a warrant for DJ's arrest.

~

Jimmy was aware that MS13 was actively recruiting members across the state of New Jersey, including right there in Atlantic City. He signed on to lend his eyes and ears to several local and federal agencies. He agreed to document any sightings or activity in his neighborhood. So far they were keeping a low profile, trying to avoid conflict with competing gangs, he guessed.

He should consider getting to know this DJ fellow. He might know the gang members that were at the picnic.

Jimmy scanned the crowd looking for DJ, but he was nowhere to be found.

He said goodbye to Ezee and stopped by the Seven-Eleven for a coffee on his way home.

Everyone wondered why there were no fireworks in the park that night.

Chapter 5:
The Phone Store

Working as a janitor, although he preferred being called a maintenance specialist, at an accounting firm during the day offered DJ the opportunity to work a part-time job at night as a security guard at a shuttered casino. He was babysitting an empty building. The night job offered him time and space to think, in peace and quiet. It also allowed him a chance to nap.

The night before was awful. There were no longer any doubts that his marriage was over. Still in shock that his beautiful girl, his wife was a stone- cold junkie and to top off that unwelcome news the bitch broke another one of his phones.

As tired as he was DJ woke up and got moving early. After having a cup of coffee with Ezee and apologizing for the last-minute request and thanking him for the use of his couch he walked home.

Remnants of the fight were still all over the floor. He grabbed a broom and swept up the broken glass and then mopped up the spilled alcohol.

His kids were upset. He did his best to reassure them, telling them that everything was going to be okay, but they weren't buying it. The guilt was crushing him. The look of fear in their little eyes hurt him deeply.

Deasia never came out of their bedroom.

After getting the kids dressed and braiding his little girl's hair he took the kids to Seven- Eleven for breakfast sandwiches. He hoped it would cheer them up at least a little bit before he dropped them off at school.

His son reminded him that he needed a parent to come into the school that afternoon to sign him up for baseball. He smiled at his ten-year-old and reassured him, he would be there to sign those papers, no matter what. After instructing his oldest to bring his younger sister and brother to the gym with him after school, he hugged them goodbye and watched as they ran into the same elementary school he went to as a kid.

Somehow he needed to find time to get himself another new phone.

Driving by the phone store on his way to work he noticed they would be open until 9:00 pm. He decided he would stop there on his way home from work.

His day job was one he liked. He was learning about investing money and saving. If only he could act on what he was learning. He always was one dollar away from going completely under no matter how hard he tried.

During the last two years all he was able to stash in savings was $5000, which was a miracle if you knew his wife.

The plan was once he had $10,000 saved he'd be able to start an investment portfolio. That was his next goal. Regardless of what was going on with his marriage, he had to do right by his kids. No if's and's or but's he was determined his kids would go to college.

He left work a little early and stopped by the house to see if Deasia was there. She would still be furious with him. There was no sign of her. As he walked back out to his car he called his mother to ask if she would watch the kids that night if he needed her. Grateful that she agreed, he headed back to the school.

Surprisingly, Deasia was standing in front of the school with Magda. “We have to sign James up for baseball.” He told her. Magda took off and left the couple to walk into the gym together without saying a word. They filled out the permission forms and got a copy of the practice schedule.

DJ dropped his family off at home and went to work at the casino.

Later that night he was going stir crazy inside the casino. He walked out onto the boards and leaned on an aluminum railing, losing himself for a few minutes while watching the moonlight on the waves. It was an unusually warm late April night. People were out walking their dogs on the beach and couples walked hand in hand along the boardwalk. A few of the benches were occupied by homeless people who kept their plastic shopping bags of belongings close.

Normally the homeless would annoy him. Tonight, for some reason, he felt bad for them.

Out of the corner of his eye, he thought he saw the guy Deasia was flirting with at the picnic. He looked to his right and yes, it was without a doubt the same guy. “Raffa or whatever his name was.” DJ couldn’t remember for sure, but there he was standing fifteen feet away with two other guys. No sooner had he spotted them, the three of them turned around and walked down the wooden ramp and off the boardwalk, glaring at him until they reached the street.

He couldn’t help wondering if it was a coincidence or if they were watching him. Whatever it was it didn’t feel right.

Things were tough enough financially for him and now he had to drop a few hundred dollars on a new phone, and he was sure his insurance wouldn’t cover the entire amount to replace his car. It was a relief they were paying for a rental but that wouldn’t last

The store was crowded so he walked around stopping to check out the newer models on display.

One of the two young ladies on duty approached him. “What are you looking for?” She asked. Handing her his shattered phone he said, “I need a replacement.”

She showed him several of the newer I-Phones and then checked his account to see if he was eligible for an upgrade. He wasn’t but she assured him that he indeed did have insurance. She showed him the model his insurance would cover, and he agreed that one would work out fine. The other young lady on duty offered to set up the new phone for him, while the girl he was working with would cash him out.

He watched the girl setting up his new phone. She was cute. Too young for him, but cute none the less. He enjoyed flirting with both.

The girl cashing him out took a picture of the computer screen. “That’s weird,” He thought, but he went right back to watching the prettier girl.

The two girls were working well together. “The way it should be.” He thought to himself. He was happy they were moving the process along because he was exhausted and had no idea what he was in for when he got home.

Thinking about home, he became annoyed.

Finally, he was handed his new phone and a bag that had a box that held his new charger, contract, his receipt, and a small book on the new phone.

Relieved that his kids were still awake he spoke with each of them, fixed them a snack, and tucked them into their beds.

He went downstairs into the kitchen, opened the refrigerator, and reached for a beer. Deasia walked into the kitchen and said, “Don’t even talk to me," then turned and walked up the stairs. She closed their bedroom door, loudly.

Honoring her wishes he went into the living room and passed out on the couch.

While he slept, Deasia called 911 and claimed her husband hit her, again.

He woke up to four of Atlantic City's finest staring at him, with their hands on their weapons. They already had a warrant, so he was handcuffed, arrested, and taken to jail.

~

After the phone store closed, the salesgirl that cashed DJ out walked to a local bar and met with a Russian friend. He ordered her a drink, and she produced a list with the personal information of fifty of the store's customers. He bought the salesperson another drink, handed her $250 and said, "I'll see you next week.

After more bar stops he went home and spent the entire night uploading the latest identification information to a server in Ukraine. Once the upload was verified he would receive $20 in Bitcoin for every name provided.

Eventually, the list would be broken down into those with good credit and those with poor credit. The Ukrainian cell would then sell both sets of information off to the highest bidders on the illegal market.

Chapter 6:
The IRS

Ezee came to his neighbor's rescue and bailed him out of jail. DJ didn't dare call his mother. Hearing the details of his accident was too much for her. This would be worse. Although she was well- aware of his marital issues he was sure knowing it escalated to this extreme would scare her.

"She threw your stuff out, it's on the side of your house. Apparently that gang banger spent the night at your house. Hate to tell you bro but rumor has it she owes drug dealers money, serious money. Eventually they're going to kill her, or you if they don't get paid."

It crossed DJ's mind more than once that his wife would consider having him killed to collect on a life insurance policy. They bought the policies when she was pregnant with their second child. He hated thinking like that, but his wife loved her drugs and money much more than she loved him or their kids. It was becoming increasingly obvious every day.

Ezee pulled up to DJ's house. Deasia's car wasn't there so he went inside.

A public defender finally called him and suggested he plead guilty, apologize, and agree to the restraining order his wife asked. DJ pleaded his case to the attorney, explaining he never laid a hand on his wife, and he never would. Even after telling this guy his wife was a junkie, he still insisted the guilty plea would get him in and out of the courtroom with no jail time.

There was no way he was ever going to admit he hit his wife ever. Forget the gang, his mother would kill him.

Frustrated DJ hung up on him.

Ezee suggested he come over to his mom's house for dinner. He also suggested DJ talk to his friend Jimmy. "The cop?" DJ shouted. "He may be able to help DJ, come on at least hear him out. He knows about this kind of stuff."

The last thing Jimmy wanted to do was talk to this guy but as a favor to his friend, he agreed.

Fausta was thrilled to have company. So was Benny.

After dessert and coffee, the three men took second cups of coffee and went out to the screened in porch, off the kitchen.

Ezee explained to Jimmy everything that happened.

"You need to plead not guilty and request a trial. They may grant her the restraining order in the meantime, but it'll give you time to get a real attorney, gather some evidence and hopefully allow everyone to calm the hell down."

This was not the advice DJ expected from a cop. What he was saying made sense.

"Thanks man. That's exactly what I'm gonna do."

His phone rang. It was the public defender. In front of Ezee and Jimmy, DJ took the advice and firmly told the attorney what he intended to do. His phone buzzed. He asked the public defender to hold on and clicked over to the next call.

"Donald Davis?" DJ froze. Nobody calls him Donald. There isn't anyone, at least less than a handful of people who know his real name. "Call me DJ?" He answered. "This is Steven Ferris from the IRS office in Philadelphia. I'm calling to inform you that the IRS has issued a warrant for your arrest." Shaking DJ asked, "For what?" Right away DJ was skeptical. This dude had a foreign accent, and he had no idea what he could have done. Except claiming he put $25 a week in the basket at church every week, when he only went to church on Christmas and Easter. Oh God do they arrest people for that?

"The warrant is for several years of tax evasion, false reporting on your income tax returns." "I don't do my own income tax returns. I get them done at a check cashing place." DJ was shaking. What the hell else could go wrong in my life!"

"Is there any way I can fix this and get the warrant dropped," DJ pleaded. "Sure Mr. Davis. Let me ask you a few questions. To make sure I have the right person are the last four of your social security number 5643, is your address 1013 Sunset Avenue?" "Yeah." "Can you confirm the rest of your social security number and birthdate?

When Jimmy overheard DJ giving his whole social security number, full name, birthdate and starting to give the routing number and account number for his checking account, he slapped the phone out of DJ's hand. "Man, who are you giving that information to?" "The IRS why?" DJ yelled. Ezee and Jimmy replied in unison. "It's a scam!"

"DJ when you were locked up for domestic violence did the cops call you and say, hey we're on our way to pick you up, no they show up without any warning."

"The guy did have an Indian accent and told me his name was Steven." DJ said, feeling ridiculous.

The next morning at the accounting office, he shared what happened with a few coworkers. "Man, DJ you did get scammed. The IRS don't call people like that. They show up at your house in blue cars, in blue suits and arrest your ass and even that rarely happens. They audit you and offer you payment arrangements. All they want is for you to pay!" Disbelieving his coworkers DJ explained how real it sounded. "Dude, you need to get to an ATM machine and check your account.

He grabbed his keys and drove the one block to the Seven- Eleven Store.

Standing in front of the ATM machine with a long line of people in line behind him, he stood there looking down at the slip of paper telling him his bank account balance was zero.

His bank branch was closed so he went back to work. Embarrassed by his own stupidity he was hoping the accountants would be able to tell him what to do.

Think back, where have you been lately? Where have you given any personal information, like your phone number or address? DJ shook his head. He couldn't remember doing anything like that, other than that phone call and he still wasn't buying that was a scam.

Then it dawned on him. It had to be Deasia and her gangster boyfriend getting back at him. They were following him and shooting at him. They knew where he worked. She's the only one that could've plotted something like this.

Still stunned DJ listened as his coworkers told him to immediately sign up for a credit protection service. That way if anyone applies for credit or opens an account in your name, the service will ping you.

His head hurt so bad. Why could he never get a break, ever?

His coworkers stressed that he needed to go to his bank first thing in the morning and to sign up for that credit protection service as soon as possible.

"Fifteen million people a year have their identity and their data breached," Berch, one of the financial advisors explained, "You'd be shocked to know how little these thieves are paid. It's like a dollar for a social security number. Debit card numbers are worth more, depending on whether the CVV and bank number are available they are worth between five and one hundred and ten dollars. Banking information, routing and account numbers are worth two hundred dollars. If it's determined the limits are too low or the victim has poor credit the information is resold, sometimes repeatedly. These thieves also get paid for driver's license numbers, your store loyalty account information and subscription account information. What's even scarier is your medical records are worth a thousand dollars and a passport is worth two thousand dollars."

DJ took his phone out and started searching information protection services. He ordered an international service on the advice of another coworker, Rob.

Rob went on to say, "You have petty thieves gathering ten or so social security numbers by digging through your trash and selling them on the web to support drug habits and then you have international organizations that have networks with cells all over the world gathering millions of pieces of personal data by putting skimmers in ATM machines and gas pumps or by using employees at smaller retail stores like convenience stores and gas stations to copy your information and selling it to support their violence. The way these networks are set up, it's impossible to stop them. They may nab a guy here and there but there's always someone else to take the place."

Berch followed up, "Then there's health insurance fraud. They steal your insurance information and file fraudulent claims. Unbelievably identity theft is one of the most common crimes reported to the FTC."

"My damn money." He was practically sobbing as he drove home from the casino.

Looking in the rearview mirror, before switching lanes he noticed a car tailgating him, close. From the best he could tell there were three men in the car. They revved the engine, passed him, and then pulled directly in front of him and slowed down. DJ nearly hit them. He pulled over and breathed a sigh of release when they floored it and moved on.

"Taking my life savings wasn't enough for them!" He shouted, pounding on his steering wheel.

His coworkers never mentioned he should go to the authorities about the identity theft. He would've never considered it either. He was too embarrassed. He went back and forth. He wasn't so sure. Should he go to the cops?

That thought went right out of his head. Of course, he wasn't going to see any cops for any kind of help. They wouldn't help him anyway, especially after all the harassment they gave him over the accident, acting like it was all his fault. "Those bastards would throw me in jail again. They profile my people. Everyone knows it's 99%!"

Playing it safe he camped out on Ezee's couch again.

Ezee handed his neighbor a beer and flipped the T.V. on.

"This guy ain't playing." Ezee said as they watched a clip of President Trump vowing to throw every MS13 member out of the country.

DJ thought about it for a second and said, "I don't agree with much of anything the orange man says but this I can get behind. I hope he succeeds in getting every one of those thugs. That I would love to see. You might even be able to get me to vote for his ass if he pulls this off!"

They clinked their beer bottles and laughed.

The next news segment was a consumer warning not to give out any identifying information over the phone. A panel discussed the IRS scam.

“How could I be so stupid.” DJ mumbled to himself. The panel offered him little hope that he would ever see his money again. Even worse was the fact that these criminals continue to do what they do because they don’t get caught.

Chapter 7:
The Victim

Deasia appeared in the courtroom the next morning with a fresh black eye and a split lip. She also produced photos of the destruction she caused in their home and blamed it on DJ Sitting behind her were several of her girlfriends including Magda and there must have been at least ten gang members. They took every opportunity to intimidate DJ by staring him down.

It went the way Jimmy said it would go. Deasia was granted her restraining order and they were told a trial date would be set.

DJ left the courthouse and went straight to a divorce attorney, one Jimmy recommended, and he filed. He also requested an emergency custody hearing.

Two days later a family court judge awarded DJ full custody of his children with Deasia getting visitation on Wednesdays and Saturday's.

Still not willing to give up completely on his marriage or at the very least getting the mother of his children the help she needed for her sake and for the kids, DJ tried calling her for two days. With no answer from her he lost his temper and went back to the phone store and cancelled her phone for good, knowing she would be furious. Illogically he did it anyway because he thought at least it would get her home. If she were here in front of him he could try again to get her to agree to going to rehab and then they could forget all this annoying restraining order and divorce stuff.

Unexpected full custody of the kids was a huge win but getting a childcare schedule together so he wouldn't miss any work was a struggle. He got it done. Once again he owed his mother, his neighbor and Ezee's wife so much. The three of them stepped up and DJ knew his kids were in great hands.

The kids did miss their mother, but DJ noticed how much calmer, even happier they seemed. "There's no drama," He thought to himself. "We hurt them with all the fighting, I have no doubt." It was good to see the joy back in their little faces, but it was hard for him to let go of the guilt he felt.

~

Pulling into his empty driveway, he wondered where his mother's car was. Everything had been going smoothly until Deasia went MIA. Not only was she not returning his calls now she missed a Saturday and the following Wednesday visit with the kids. This caused DJ to rely on his mother even more. Where was his mother now, it was late, it was late? This wasn't like her.

He dialed her number.

"Deasia picked them up a few hours ago," His mother said, "She told me you knew."

"Maybe she got a ride back and is in the house with them." he thought.

Checking the kitchen first, the living room and then each of the kid's rooms, there was no sign of them. The house was eerily quiet and empty. It was late, where could they be. His mind went right to worst case scenario. One of the kids was sick or hurt, they could've been in an accident.

"I shut her friggin phone off and now she couldn't even call me if she wanted too!" He shouted.

"Or she was gone taking my kids with her." Panic set in.

He called Magda. "What the hell DJ I have no damned idea where she is, I haven't seen her all day."

He had the strongest of feelings that she was lying but there was nothing he could do about it, not now.

There was nothing he could do about anything this late at night and he was so tired. Knowing in his heart Deasia would never hurt their kids, he took a shower and went to bed.

Nearly breaking his neck jumping or it was falling out of bed, he got as low as he could on the floor. Struggling to decide if what woke him from a sound sleep was shattering glass or gunfire, he crawled along the floor to the other side of his bed, away from the window.

Whatever was going on it was extremely close to home. "Am I in the middle of a nightmare or is this reality?" He reached up onto the night table for his phone. 3:38 AM. "What the hell?" He thought.

Fully awake and stone cold aware of the fact that whatever or whoever it was, it was about him.

The sound of screeching tires got further away, and the shrill sound of sirens got closer, so he slowly got up and went to the front window. Carefully he lifted a bottom slat on the mini blind and slowly peaked. He didn't see anyone. "What the hell," he said to himself again. Crawling back into bed, he put the interruption of much needed sleep out of his mind and fell back to sleep for a whole five minutes.

Someone was pounding on his front door. Through the sidelights he could see flashing lights. "Who's there?" He yelled. "Police Mr. Davis please open the door now!"

He barely had the front door open, and two cops barreled into his living room. "What's going on?" DJ asked. "Your car windows were smashed. Didn't you hear it? Did you see anything? Do you have any enemies? We had numerous calls. Your neighbors weren't sure if it was gunfire or glass."

Stunned, DJ stood there shaking his head. "My car?" He mumbled. He started to walk towards the front door but one of the officers stopped him. "We aren't sure it's secure enough for you to go outside."

"My wife may be cheating on me. I'm not even sure where she is, where my kids are. I saw the guy she's been seeing. He was by my job with two other guys. It didn't seem right." Putting his head down, he decided he said way too much.

He didn't trust these guys and honestly he was waiting for them to throw him against the wall and arrest him for beating on his own car.

His whole life he dealt with it, well not so much him personally but he'd heard so many stories of state sanctioned police violence against Black people. His people! For the past couple of years, he'd been researching and studying police involved shootings, the statistics, and racial profiling. He wanted a different world for his kids, a fully liberated life free from profiling, free from systemic racism.

All his talk of justice and liberation scared his mother. She said it was distracting him, making him too angry and she continued to tell him his attitude was becoming ruder and more disrespectful. "Anger is like a brick wall," she would tell him, "You can't move forward until you knock that wall down. If you need to, one brick at a time."

As a kid DJ often got himself into trouble with the law. It started small, stealing candy, getting into fights, and elevated to him stealing a car when he was fifteen.

His mother made it loud and clear to him that if he didn't clean up his act; apply himself in school and focus on graduating the next time he was arrested; she would leave him there for good.

There was no doubt in his mind, at that time she meant every word.

Once he started focusing and became more involved in school he made new friends, one of them Deasia.

That night, in his living room he was seriously considering his mother's words.

She was always there for him. Tough as nails but she was also his biggest supporter. While he was growing up she worked at the Trump Casino. She started as a cashier and worked her way up to becoming an administrative assistant to one of the account executives.

When that casino closed, his mom was disappointed but relieved she was able to retire with a full pension and her 401K.

As tough as she was, DJ was always proud of her. It was still weird to think about this guy she worked for all those years ago was now the President of the United States. His mother always looked up to and admired the man. She refused to believe he changed after he sold his interest in the casino. No matter how hard he tried DJ he could not make her see what a creep he believed he was now, and always had been.

~

"Are you okay Mr. Davis?" One of the officers asked. Pulling himself together and doing his best to shake off his attitude he answered their questions, the best he could.

His elderly neighbor, Sophie came in and sat with him while the police finished their report. Once they left she helped him sweep up the broken glass.

"I thought someone hurt you," She started, "I was so scared." DJ hugged her, thanked her, and walked her to her front door. "Lock your doors and windows." She told him, "And don't answer the door for anyone." She said as she patted his cheek. "You do the same, Sophie and try to get some sleep. I'm sorry you were scared."

By the time he got back into bed the sun was coming up. He set his alarm for 8:15. That would give him plenty of time to get a quick shower and something to eat.

~

While eating a bowl of Cap'n Crunch he called the phone store and had Deasia's phone turned back on. The guy on the other end of the phone said to give him fifteen minutes to get it working. Fifteen minutes passed slowly, and DJ while gritting his teeth left as nice a message as he could manage, asking his wife to please call him.

With every window busted out of his rental car, and shattered glass covering the seats and floor he decided to call for a tow truck and an Uber. Would he be in trouble with the car rental company? Would his insurance cover this mess? Will they supply another rental car? How long will all this take? One thing was for sure, he was going to be on the phone most of the day. Luckily, that wouldn't be a problem at either of his jobs.

"Who'd you piss off?" The tow truck operator asked. DJ wanted to knock him out. His Uber driver arrived just on time.

He had to get to the bank. His boss wasn't happy he would be late, but he had to do what he had to do.

The lobby was crowded. Frustration was getting harder to suppress and he was thinking about leaving when they finally called his name. He followed a woman who introduced herself as Kimberly into her glass partitioned cubicle.

As he told her the story, she never took her eyes off her computer screen. Once he finished talking, she looked up and asked him if his wife could've taken the money. "No, it wasn't her. I told you I got that phony IRS scam call. It was them. MS13 was behind the call.

"There will be an investigation so for now the safest thing for you to do is to close your bank accounts, cancel all of your debit and credit cards and open new accounts."

"Will I ever get my money back?" he asked Kimberly. "We'll do our best." She said as she smiled one of those sorry not sorry smiles at him.

With the last twenty dollars in cash, he had in his wallet, he opened a new checking account so he could at least have his paychecks direct deposited. It seemed to take forever for her to get the new account set up and he was becoming angrier with each passing minute.

Finally, she handed him his new check book, ATM card and a bunch of paperwork on fraud and how the bank handled investigations.

He called both his employers to give them his new account number. Hopefully, it wasn't too late! If his pay checks were delayed he'd be royally screwed.

At the office he found a corner and sat down to make calls to the body shop, his credit card companies, the rental car company and he tried Deasia, again. No answer. "Where the hell is she and where are my kids?" He was getting nervous.

When his shift was over he had his Uber driver ride by the school. There was no sign of his wife or the kids. "Damn it. They can't be missing school!"

Back at his house, he made a sandwich and was standing out front waiting for his ride when he got a text saying his ride and his credit card were cancelled. "Damn!" Ezee walked up behind him, startling him at first.

“What the hell happened man?” “I honestly don’t know Ezee, but I also been scammed of my money, and I need a ride to work.” His neighbor obliged.

Ezee was a bit surprised. “Jimmy caught you on that call before you gave any pertinent information. How did they get it?” “That call screwed everything up so fast. It’s that gang and my bitch of a wife. Nothing else makes sense.

“Shoot me a text if you need a ride home tonight.” Thanks, Ezee, thanks man.”

There were issues at the casino that kept him busy from the moment he arrived. Someone broke in during the day, so his boss decided to do rounds with him.

He missed a call. It was from the body shop. The damage to his rental car was covered by his home- owners insurance. There was a deductible of course and they would supply another rental car. The repairs would take three days.

Now he’d have to wait until morning to make the arrangements for a new rental car.

Ezee gave him a ride home.

After calling everyone he could think of that might know where Deasia was, he put on the end of a basketball game and fell asleep on the couch.

“Not again,” He mumbled as he awoke to every dog in the neighborhood barking. Someone was banging on his sliding door. Half asleep he stumbled through the kitchen. He could see a shadow through the blinds. Struck with panic, he walked with his back along the wall and moved one of the slats on the blinds ever so slightly.

A man with a gun was standing there. His eyes were glowing, and DJ could see him grinning. He stumbled and fell backwards. Jumping up he hurried to put his back against the wall, away from the window. Watching through the open slat on the blinds he saw the shadows of two more men run by.

He slid down along the wall until he was sitting on the floor. He spent the rest of the night there, on the floor sleeping on and off.

Startled awake again, this time by someone banging on his front door. By the time he made it to the front door, whoever it was had gone. His phone rang and he jumped. There was no one there either.

"FUCK YOU MOTHER FUCKERS. I GOT SOMETHING FOR YOU. COME ON IN! He screamed hoping they would believe he was armed and decide not to break in. He paced up and down his foyer for what seemed like forever. He wanted to open the door, to check but decided that was a bad idea.

After going back and forth with himself on whether he should call the police, he decided not to. He didn't feel safe talking to anyone but knew he'd have to tell someone. Wondering if they were only trying to scare him or if they were trying to kill him was terrifying and it was making him paranoid. "Paranoid people make mistakes." He said to himself over, and over again.

Should he confide in his mother? Was it time? She would be furious with him at first for keeping everything from her and then she'd be scared to death. But could she do anything to help. No, he decided. If he left it up to her she would call the damned cops and he was sure if that happened he'd be dead for sure.

Chapter 8:
MS13

After going round and round with Magda on the phone, DJ finally got her to admit that Deasia and the kids were okay. "They're fine DJ, but they're gone. She's not coming back." The pain he felt when she said, *they're gone* was so overwhelming he couldn't find the words to describe exactly where it hurt. It was sharp, deep, and everywhere. He was nauseas. The worry and devastation was consuming him.

~

Maria had plans with her girlfriends, so Jimmy decided to make an appearance at another one of Ezee's parties. This time the get together was at Ezee's house. Jimmy figured it would be a good chance to pick up on the latest gang related gossip.

Jimmy was well known in Atlantic City but personally, he kept a small close circle of friends. One such friend, Frank the FBI agent, recently asked him to keep his eyes and ears open for any intel on MS13 activity. Frank and Jimmy were anything but friends when they first met in an office at the Atlantic City Police Station.

It was Frank that cleared Jimmy when he was falsely accused of being a bad cop by Tommy. During that investigation Jimmy found out that the director of the FBI, Frank's boss was one of the FBI agents that conducted a less than up and up investigation that sent Jimmy's Dad to jail ending his thirty plus year political career. The move was in retaliation for nearly unseating a long-term Congressman. The Congressman won the election by a slim margin of 1500 votes. Over a million votes were cast.

The rumor was that the congressman had the FBI and IRS investigate until they found something, anything to rid Jimmy's Dad as a threat. It seemed Jimmy and DJ were a lot more alike when it came to trusting people in authority. Jimmy's Dad was no stranger to Atlantic City politics. Back then he helped the Atlantic City Council and Mayor, Mayor Usry to set the city up administratively. It had just passed casino gaming and they had no idea what was going to be heading their way in the form of land development, builders, jobs, and a phenomenal increase in tax and other city revenue money.

When Jimmy retired, a group of political activists asked him to get involved in local politics. He was able to fundamentally change the format of city elections giving the advantage to a large majority of African American partisan voters. He also amassed a large voter base of Vietnamese, Chinese, Bangladesh, Pakistan, Arabs, and Korean residents. This block of voters made Jimmy a king maker. His base was large enough to swing any city-wide election. It wasn't enough to get him into the mayor's office because he would have to make deals with those that make the government political, anti-user friendly and corrupt. He chose the lesser evil knowing no matter who he helped they could turn against him and what he stood for.

For example, an election where Jimmy was asked not to run by the very person that cost him an earlier run for office by submitting fraudulent absentee ballots. Later in the general election, enough of those ballots were proven fraudulent that would have had Jimmy win by fifty votes in the primary and easily wining the general election because no other candidate generated the amount of votes Jimmy did. This person was now the President of City Council and was running for mayor.

This Council President was a cooperating witness for the FBI due to charges they had hanging over his head. He was wearing a wire trying to ensnare others he felt should get locked up too. If he was going down, he was taking others with him.

The problem was not that no one knew, the problem was he was going to win if he had Jimmy's support. The FBI told him he had to step down before the election. He got some alcoholic with plenty of his own skeletons to run, with the understanding that certain shady political players would be doing the job and all he would have to do would be to 'cut ribbons and kiss babies.'

After unseating the long-term mayor and replacing him with a white alcoholic in a prominently Black favored electorate solidified Jimmy's place in Atlantic City as a political powerbroker. One to be hated by those of the deep state. Jimmy was given a position as the Director of Neighborhood Services which controls all construction and regulations as well as licensing of businesses in the city. A position coveted by the deep state for its ability to provide massive amounts of kickbacks and bribes. It was the parting shot from the City council president to those that were not caught up in the legal firestorm. They weren't going to jail but their gravy train came to a screeching halt.

Everyone knew Jimmy would not ignore wrongdoing or bribery and he would clean up the corruption running rampant in that department.

It didn't take long for Jimmy to see he was out gunned by politicians, big money, and unions. They had their hooks in deep with his inspectors who began delaying construction jobs. No bigger example was the Caesar's Pier project. The contractor was being crushed by inspectors changing their minds on what they approved saying it had to be done another way which would cost millions of dollars. The builder would have to undue work that had been done, and redo it another way with no legitimate safety or health reason for the changes. Jimmy knowing if he went to the police department, they would tip off the inspectors. Several of the inspectors had family members who had long ties with unions and politicians who received huge campaign contributions and cushy no-show jobs. So, Jimmy reached out to Frank for help. Jimmy never thought he would use the business card Frank gave him. He was glad he hung on to the card.

Jimmy called his secretary and personal assistant. He told them he was closing his office door and he was not to be disturbed until he opened it. He dialed the number and by the third rang he knew he would be leaving a message but on the fourth ring Frank picked up responding Agent Furhman. Jimmy said, "Frank" the Agent responded, "Yes, who am I speaking to." Jimmy answered, "James Tayborn from Atlantic City." Frank replied, "Oh Yes, what can I do for you." Jimmy said, "I've taken a position in the Barsky administration. I met with a casino developer who wanted to know if I could help him cut through some red tape and help him to get his project done. He estimated the project to cost seventy-five million dollars and it was now at 225 million dollars. This is loud and clear that I'm dealing with more than cost overruns. I have two inspectors going out in the morning, guys I trust. I asked them to inspect the change suggestions and to decipher if they were needed for health and safety reasons. If they decide the changes weren't needed for health and safety reasons I would be able to terminate the original inspector. The developer's subcontractors are speaking out about shake downs for cash or equipment before they will pass the work."

Frank thought for a few minutes and responded, "Why don't you go through the police department?" Jimmy becoming aggravated said, "They put the Chief's nephew Micky in charge of Mercantile. The problem is he's still working for the police department. He claims he doesn't have to answer to me since he's still active with the force and therefore is assigned under the Chief. We're talking about $150 million dollars in bribes here. This involves interstate corporations and products so it falls under your authority if you think you can find some wrongdoing out of the extra 150 million dollars this developer has already spent."

Jimmy was getting heat from politicians, unions, and the administration because of the actions he was taking. The Caesar's Pier did open on time and the developer met his deadlines for the financing he needed to pay to his debtors. Two weeks after the opening Frank came and met with Jimmy.

He apologized for his failure in getting things into place. He told Jimmy that there was so much more than what he told him, and he was unable to put a team in place quick enough. Frank was frustrated because he trusted that the FBI was above the fray. He now understood Jimmy's apprehension of trusting the chain of command due to the intermingling of corruption between all the agencies.

Jimmy could read the disappointment and anger Frank was trying to suppress. Frank assured Jimmy that going forward he too would be playing and keeping things closer to the vest.

Jimmy said "Well maybe you can do better with this one. This city has two hundred and fifty licensed cabs. By law you're only allowed to have two drivers per licensed cab. If you do the math that a maximum of five hundred drivers. The Mercantile department that issues these licenses has issued two thousand fifty-seven licenses so far this year. It has also come to my attention that these and other licenses like rolling chair operators, cab, limo licenses are being issued for a fee of $5000 each. Doing the math this means there is over $7,500,000 million dollars in bribe money going into a lot of peoples, pockets. It explains to me why the personnel that I transferred magically were reassigned back to their positions by the business administrator and why he is now filing charges against me. I don't know how much longer I am going to be here."

Frank said, "I can give you some state contacts, but I don't see how this is Federal Jim?"

Jimmy said, "Frank, I'm not telling you all this to waste my time. My contacts in the middle eastern communities are telling me that we are being overrun by enemy combatants and not just any combatants they are trained insurgent groups, military destabilization strike teams and terrorist recruiting teams."

Frank said, "Woah! How did we get here from Mercantile licenses?" Jimmy said, "I asked myself the same question. I was told if you sneak across the United States border there isn't much you can do legally as an illegal. You can however be used in any number of illegal ways. You could be hired to physically attack someone, plant a bomb, unknowingly or God forbid knowingly blow yourself up, or most importantly gather information. But, if you're here on a work visa you can get a driver's license, open a bank account, get a plane ticket, put money in that bank account, and so many other critical things legally. You may even receive a mail-in ballot and be able to vote!

To obtain that work visa, they must show where they are working and there is a limited number of companies that will hire them. These companies are under constant scrutiny and often go out of business. What better proof that you as a foreigner who has obtained work on your visa than a City of Atlantic City License to do business in the city. They are rarely reviewed and now we know it's because they run in to a $7,500,000 dead-end supported by a large group of city workers so they can keep their money flowing. My sources are telling me these foreigners are from Iraq, Iran, and Pakistan."

The day Jimmy planned to revoke every Atlantic City cab license that had more than two licensed drivers registered he was asked by the Police Chiefs nephew to wait until he returned from a trip. Jimmy agreed and the two of them agreed the licenses would be revoked the following Wednesday.

When he arrived to work that Wednesday the business administrator was waiting for him and asked him to go the mayor's office. Upon entering the mayor's office, the mayor said nervously, "Good you are here." He then handed Jimmy an envelope which contained a letter saying, "Thank You for your service and we have no more need for you." Jimmy said, "You really want to end it this way?" The mayor didn't answer so Jimmy said again, "Are you sure this is how you want to end this?" The mayor mumbled, "The letter says it all." The mayor was cut off by the Business Administrator saying, "don't say nothing." Jimmy went down to his office on the fifth floor where the Chief's nephew was waiting for him. Jimmy's Secretary was just getting into the office. The Chief's nephew Micky Booser said, "When do you want to do this thing?" Jimmy said. "I don't know. You must bring it up with the Business Administrator, I was just fired." At the same time the Secretary yelled "No!" Micky said, "I know. I just wanted to see your face when you said the words, I was fired."

Two weeks later, Frank with a crew of twelve agents served a search warrant on the City's Mercantile Office pulling boxes and boxes, filling up three vans. Jimmy filed a whistleblower lawsuit and despite the mayor, who fired him being charged for one of the skeletons in his closet, the case would drag on.

Frank showed up on Jimmy's doorstep. When Maria answered the door, he would not say who he was. He only told her he needed to give Jimmy some information, and if anyone spotted him doing so, he would lose his job. Maria invited him in to wait for Jimmy. When Jimmy got home, Frank told him how spot on his sources were about the Mercantile Office. The FBI was only aware of and only tracking 15% of the terrorists on your list. Frank told Jimmy to be extremely careful.

Those in that department are terrified of going to jail, or worse being killed because the terrorist will cover their tracks, which is a fact. Jimmy knew Frank was risking his job by sharing this information with him.

Frank revealed that the decision was made to keep a lid on all of this so they could keep tracking the terrorists. The FBI did enact searches at airports based on intel they were receiving on detailed planned attacks. We did the searches randomly because we didn't want the terrorists to know how much we knew about them.

Jimmy they are already talking about killing you, but we sent them some disinformation to hopefully throw them off.

"BUT!" Jimmy screamed. Frank cut him off and said, "Your lawsuit is not going anywhere. We will try to work out a settlement for you because I know you planned on that salary for at least four years, but the lawsuit will never see the light of day."

Jimmy screamed again, "WHO!" "It's the director." Frank answered. "I wanted to lock up a bunch of low- lying fruit that wouldn't compromise what we have going on because God knows this City needs a good flushing, but it's not my call."

Jimmy was frustrated. He said, "Frank, I know the risk you're taking to tell me this, but it doesn't make me feel better. I know I can't do anything about it, but I need you to promise me if I ever call you, you will have my back and I'll do the same for you." Frank said, "I consider you one of the good guys so that makes us in this together, so as a friend if you need me to look into something I will."

Shortly after that conversation, Frank asked Jimmy to attend an FBI/Homeland Security Joint Taskforce on MS13 and gang violence briefing. Frank greeted Jimmy at the door of the FBI Headquarters and escorted him to the conference room. Jimmy had taken part in multiple joint task force investigations in that same conference room. At one time it was like a second home to him. If he was being honest it felt a bit strange being there again.

Frank and Jimmy signed in and took a seat in the conference room. Looking around the room Jimmy only recognized a few local police officers, and a few of the federal agents.

The District FBI Director, Senior Agent Sean McKean walked into the room and asked if Frank would come to his office. Frank got up and asked Jimmy to save his seat.

Frank knocked on the open door of the Director's office. McKean was looking through what looked to Frank like an old file. He told Frank to come in and close the door. "Yes Sir, what can I do for you" Frank asked. The Director said, "I see you brought in a civilian advisor on this MS13 intel briefing." Yes Sir, is there an issue? Jimmy is a highly decorated Atlantic City Police Officer who was injured in the line of duty." The Director responded, "But you were in charge of the investigation into him intimidating a neighbor into selling her home." Frank said, "All due respect Director like Jimmy said to me, if you had a crack house across the street from your home, you would do whatever you could to get the authorities to enforce any law or building code that was being violated. Jimmy exhausted every legal course to force the absentee landlord to keep up the maintenance on the property and to keep out the people who were destroying the property and neighborhood. He filed a complaint because work was being done without permits and the Trust Fund Administrator from Washington D.C. finally decided to sell the property. Yes, Jimmy placed a full price offer and with no other offers due to the amount of work needed to bring the house up to code his offer was finally accepted. It cost Jimmy as much as he paid for the house to bring it up to code. Jimmy was right when he said to me, I would be a liar if I could buy the crack house across the street from my house and didn't. He did nothing wrong. The complainant, who was not even the absentee owner of the property but a dirty cop who was Jimmy's partner on a drug bust who falsely accused Jimmy of being a dirty cop. When we let Jimmy know, it was his currently assigned partner who made the complaint, Jimmy informed us that this cop bragged about being able to amass over a million dollars stealing drug money. That dirty cop has been involved in many of our Joint investigations and we were able to start putting the accounting errors reported during the time with the amounts in his bank account. The numbers matched equally. After retiring the city hired Jimmy to oversee the Neighborhood Services Department. His responsibility was to oversee all construction and building licenses. We didn't act fast enough on information we were getting from him, on the corruption that goes on in that city. Before we could act, they asked him to resign. He was able to give us the information contained in FAR2006-A1-743. That information alone has kept the Country safe from multiple terrorist plots and attacks. To this day that intel continues to keep us ahead of the multiple cells running in the United States, specifically on the Eastern Coast. I only feel bad that we had to bury his whistleblower lawsuit, so we didn't expose the intel contained in FAR2006-A1-743.

The Director thought for a minute and replied, "That was this guy? Now I know how the old Director got promoted to D.C. I never understood why they promoted that guy. He was the one that came up with the stupid idea to make us wait in those long lines and take our shoes off in airports."

Frank said, "We were able to nab forty-five foreign trained operatives before they entered flights. He didn't want to let the bad actors know we knew who they were, so we had to make the searches appear random.

Jimmy was involved in the intel that led to those arrests. He is trustworthy, I give you my word. He also turned in other terrorist cells with links to friends of his, one guy was in his wedding. Because of our intervention, we put out some misleading information, so Jimmy is still in touch with that guy. he is still in contact with them thanks to our intervention with some miss information. Because of that our wire taps we were able to pick up information that they wanted to kill Jimmy. So, if he says he can get us local intel on MS13 in the Atlantic City area one of the largest gateways for terrorist infiltration into this country, I would be derelict of my duties not to bring him on to this Task Force. I'm proud that he accepted me as a friend especially since I investigated him hard when that complaint came from a highly respected cop, who turned out to be dirty."

The Director was now thinking that Frank might be his ace in the hole for achieving a promotion to his desired position in D.C. He started feeling like something big could come out of all this. He could get the White House to make it a top priority.

The Director asked Frank, "How come you didn't go to D.C.?" Frank answered, "The Director made it clear that my place was here. Did I mention that the dirty cop was his claim to fame? Because of all the drug busts he made on the cop's intel, he made Director" The Director then said, "Do you think you would go if the opportunity came your way again." Frank answered, "No Sir, too close to be retiring, and would not want to be caught up in the politics of D.C. It's too swampy. You never know when you will be asked to do things you know are not right just because a politician is afraid of losing their power and their spot on the gravy train."

Jimmy started to wonder what was taking Frank so long. He wondered if whatever he was doing involved him.

His thoughts wandered back to the first time he was assigned to a Joint Task Force Investigation lead by the Drug Enforcement Agency (DEA.) The investigation also included the Federal Bureau of Investigations (FBI) and the Alcohol Tobacco and Firearms (ATF.) The Task Force was working on a major drug distribution network that was transporting drugs and guns from Columbia and distributing them throughout multiple states. A major break in the case came when a guy who was not involved but he knew a lot of the players in New Jersey and North Carolina. He was an assistant line cook at a casino in Atlantic City. Jimmy stopped him for driving while his license was suspended.

Not looking to keep the guy from being able to get back and forth from work, Jimmy told the guy to pay his fines, get his license reinstated and he would help him out with the ticket he wrote him. The cook didn't follow through. Jimmy often helped good hard-working people get their driving privileges restored. But, if you did not try to help yourself Jimmy would enforce the law.

He knew those not willing to help themselves were the kind of people that would hit a person with their car and flee. People that did not care if they had insurance and did not care who they hurt because they thought they had a right to drive.

Jimmy told the assistant cook not to take his kindness for weakness that if he continued to choose not to get his license straightened out by the time he went to court that Jimmy would stop him every time he spotted him driving and he would continually to ticket him. Eventually he would end up spending time in jail and he would lose his job.

The cook failed to appear for his hearing. Jimmy stopped him leaving work at the casino. He was driving a classically restored 1980's Monte Carlo, the same car he was driving the first time Jimmy pulled him over. Jimmy said, "Well you took my kindness for weakness. At least you could have picked a less unique vehicle. I'll be making a point of looking for you and it is not that hard since you leave the same time every night. When you bail yourself out of jail you better find the bus schedule."

This assistant cook was not a criminal per say but he did think the world owed him and the law did not apply to him. After being stopped four times, being ticketed, and having his car towed resulting in thousands of dollars in fines the cook was arrested, and he lost his job. He made bail and fled the State.

Jimmy never saw him again, until that first Task Force Meeting way back when. He had always figured the guy got the same kind of work somewhere in North Carolina, where he was originally from, making a lot less money than he did at the casino.

Then years later this assistant cook for no other reason than trying to get out of going to jail for the suspended driving tickets Jimmy wrote him agreed to wear wires, buy guns, and drugs with marked money and to turn them over to the ATF and DEA was utterly amazing. This cook single handedly took a bite out of a multi-million- dollar drug and gun cartel with Columbian ties just to get himself out of the traffic ticket mess.

But now here Jimmy was a retired cop, and he was being treated like an outsider with no clearances. It was bittersweet. He hated that they didn't trust him with procedures or to preserve evidence, and the integrity of ongoing investigations.

Frank and the Director shook hands and walked into the conference room.

The Director introduced Jimmy, which made him feel more welcome and respected.

After the briefing Jimmy read everything he could find on the MS13.

It seemed new information was coming out every day, exasperated by the President's continuous mention of them during his campaign.

These savages chased and then brutally tortured and killed two teenage girls with a machete on Long Island. Their "leader" or "director" was now living somewhere in New Jersey. Not only was he living here, the criminal activity and the number of members was rapidly increasing across the entire state.

The gang members live in neighborhoods that tend to be diverse. It's getting more difficult to identify them because newer, younger members are foregoing the tattoos and the "typical" look so they blend in with their neighbors. During the day they're taking their kids to school, working as painters, landscapers and opening Mom and Pop corner stores on every corner in the city.

Once night falls their criminal behaviors are destabilizing entire communities and terrifying already frightened residents, making them less likely to report crimes.

Age wise they can be as young as thirteen, as old as eighty or anywhere in between.

Even more difficult is the task of trying to determine exactly what they do. Heroin, it's believed is their product of choice, with human trafficking close to surpassing the gangs drug business.

Some intel sources believe they also work as a sort of bail bond syndicate specializing in getting immigration offenders released. Once released some time is given to pay back the bond with outrageous interest. If payment isn't made in the specified time frame the victim is tortured and recruited to work as a slave for the organization or they are killed in a brutal, public way as an example.

It's also believed they're acting as hit men, not only for their own organization but for anyone that wants to hire them.

Another difficulty in pinpointing all the criminal activities of these guys and the female members as well is the fact that they don't do it for the money, they do it for loyalty to the family

Every criminal organization in the world that's been stopped has been brought down by their leader's own greed. They cheat on their taxes or get involved with insider trading. This allows the IRS to get involved in investigations. Financial crimes can be much easier to prove and prosecute.

For MS13 it isn't about the money, it's about the power and the glory, and most frightening is the fact that like most terrorists they are not afraid to die.

~

Jimmy walked into Ezee's living room.

"Somethings up with the guy," Ezee said to Jimmy, "Someone busted every window outta his car, woke me from a sound sleep the other night." "Who do you think it was?" Jimmy asked. "No clue. But someone don't like him"

The cop in Jimmy couldn't help digging deeper. "Is he dealing? Does he use? Does he owe someone?" "I've never known him to do either. He's straight up," Ezee said, shaking his head, "The only illegal thing I've ever known him to do is the pyro stuff. You know the illegal fireworks, and honestly he hasn't even been bothering with those."

After hesitating, Ezee mentioned DJ's wife may have left him for an MS13 member.

"Now that is interesting." Jimmy mumbled to himself.

Ezee's wife interrupted the discussion.

Jimmy scanned the rest of the living room. Not seeing anyone he knew or anyone interesting either, he walked through the dining room and fixed a drink in the kitchen. Then he made his way out into the back yard.

Everyone was dressed casually but in a nice casual way.

Walking across the stone patio he made his way to an empty chair and lit a cigar. He gave the habit up years earlier but every once in a while a smoke went so well with a drink.

"5-0 in the house." DJ said loudly as he walked by Jimmy.

"Clown." Jimmy mumbled to himself.

DJ turned around and offered his hand to Jimmy. Standing up, Jimmy shook his hand. "Thanks man for your advice with my court stuff. You were right and so far it's all working out the way you said it would." "Glad to hear it DJ let me know if there's anything else I can do."

DJ went back inside.

After learning at the FBI MS13 Task Force briefing he attended with, Frank how difficult it was to identify gang members, Jimmy looked around at the crowd in the yard and wondered what other clues he should be looking for.

A weapon in a waistband. That wouldn't necessarily mean someone was an MS13 member, it could be anyone.

Three men that fit the murky MS13 profile, gathered around the fire pit. Jimmy made his way towards them and warmed his hands over the fire. They were discussing one of them having a brand-new baby girl and then they moved on to debating at great length that afternoons Phillies loss and which players were to blame.

Remembering more of the information that was presented at that Task Force meeting, he took mental notes on each of their descriptions.

MS13 was a gang started with the intention of protecting Salvadorian immigrants from other gangs in California. They started in the 1970's and grew larger in the 1980's. Today they are the largest and one of the most violent gangs in the world. They continue to expand into more countries and continue to grow their criminal enterprises.

Law enforcement estimates there are at least 70,000 members with most members in California, North Carolina and on Long Island in New York. The numbers continue to grow in New Jersey. As the numbers grow in the state so does the gang activity.

The members themselves see the organization more as a social group then they do a criminal organization. They continue to frustrate law enforcement because of the members skills at being able to cross back and forth the southern border undetected and the inability of the law to find them. Because they have no actual infrastructure and so single leader or leaders, the gang operates without rules. This also keeps them impoverished and increasingly more violent.

It's a fact that only a small percentage of undocumented immigrants are criminals. Sadly, though with the number of MS13 members in the United States, their increasing violence sheds a dark light on all immigrants.

~

Jimmy couldn't help wondering why the Spanish thug he met at the picnic wasn't there and DJ's wife was nowhere to be found either.

After a few more beers, Jimmy walked home.

~

DJ's phone pinged. He walked into Ezee's kitchen where the light was better. It was a notice from his credit protection service letting him know someone was using his name and his credit to buy a car in Baltimore. He went into the bathroom and called the dealership. The phone rang and rang. "Damn!" He muttered. They were closed.

"This must be Deasia, what the hell is she doing in Maryland?"

There were other notices. An EZ Pass was purchased on the Pennsylvania turnpike and two credit card accounts were opened in his name. There were also notices that credit was denied at three car dealerships. This gave DJ great satisfaction; it was fleeting but felt good for a moment.

Not at all happy that his credit was now deeper in the toilet than ever because of that bitch-at least she was denied at first. The satisfaction he felt quickly turned to anger when it sunk in that in the end she did get a damned car.

No longer in the mood to party he said his goodbyes and started walking home.

Right before he reached his driveway, a rust colored, low riding Camaro slowed to a stop. DJ turned towards the car and saw a man cowering in the passenger seat with a gun pointed in his direction. "Fuck."

His feet felt like they were sinking in wet concrete. His body froze but his brain took over. He threw himself on the ground and quickly rolled behind his neighbor's trash cans as shots rang out. Grabbing an old metal trashcan lid, he held it in front of his head. He could see headlights from another car coming down the street slowly from the opposite direction.

Bullets whizzed all around him. He prayed none of his neighbors would be hit, especially Sophie.

The Camaro's tires screeched. DJ started feeling his head, shoulders and made his way down to his feet, checking to see if he'd been hit. He was soaked with sweat and trembling.

A group of people that'd been in Ezee's backyard, slowly made their way down the sidewalk to DJ He sat up and tried to catch his breath. Within minutes there were six police cars, and two ambulances. His neighbors started to peer out slightly opened front doors with phones in hand.

Once the EMT's cleared him four cops followed him into his house. The others stayed outside to question and get statements from the party goers and other neighbors.

Without saying too much, DJ told the cops again that his wife left him, and he suspected but wasn't sure if she was with an MS13 gang member.

The officers strongly suggested he pack up and find a place to stay, somewhere his wife or her new friends wouldn't consider looking for him.

He couldn't sleep. Somewhere between three and four in the morning he saw his life flash before his eyes. He sat straight up in bed. "This is NO joke." He said to himself. "They're legit trying to kill me."

Ezee showed up first thing in the morning to take DJ to pick up his new rental car. "You've got to find somewhere else to be," Ezee said, "This is out of hand. I'll ask around to see if I can find a place for you to lay low." "At least they don't know this car." DJ said. "Yet." Ezee answered.

~

Raffa insisted Deasia gather up her kids, a few belongings and go with him to Miami. They took a bus from Atlantic City to Baltimore. It was there she suggested out of desperation that they buy a car for the rest of the trip. The bus was downright hard for the kids and that made it miserable for her.

Once they finally got a yes from a dealership, they got back on I-95 and headed south. They made it as far as Richmond, Virginia and decided to stop for the night.

Deasia second guessed what she was doing, more than once but when she looked over at Raffa and watched through the crack in the bathroom door as he tucked her children into one of the two king size beds, she felt less guilty. Whatever he may be or not be, he was good with kids. They liked him.

She was starting to feel sick in the car and was relieved it would only be a few minutes longer and she would be much better.

Once she got her fix, she soaked in a warm bath. Raffa went outside into the parking lot and was on the phone for over an hour.

Deasia woke up when she heard the motel room door open. She was freezing. Raffa lifted her out of the tub, dried her off and helped her into bed.

After sleeping in, they were back on the road by 11:00 AM. Cracker Barrel was the absolute worst place to stop for breakfast with three little kids. Shuffling them through the general store to the table took several bribes including the opportunity to pick out candy and a toy for the ride, after they ate their breakfast.

~

"Who better to hide his neighbor than Jimmy," Ezee thought, "It's perfect" He'd been wracking his brain trying to think of a safe place for DJ to hide out for a few days. At least until the police could get to the bottom of these attacks on his life. Jimmy would know exactly what to do and who to call, should anything go down.

Chapter 9:
The Safe House

"That Black Lives Matter guy with the ten-pound chip on his shoulder?" Jimmy couldn't believe what Ezee was asking him to do. "He's a freaking clown!"

"He did take your advice about court and Jimmy these dudes aren't fucking around. They're gonna take him out, it's only a matter of time before his nine-lives run out or worse, the poor neighbors get caught in the crossfire." Ezee reminded him.

Contemplating the pros and cons Jimmy thought it might be a good way to get real first- hand intel and he did have a fully functional kitchen and bathroom in the showroom. There was also a changing room that could serve as a bedroom All he had to do was set up a cot in there.

"Okay I'll help him, but he can stay at the shop not in my house."

MS13 was stepping up their violent attacks in New Jersey and if this idiot could help in any way he didn't have any other choice than to put DJ up and keep him safe for however long it might take.

Maria was dead set against the idea. Once they convinced her it truly was a matter of life and death, and they couldn't sit back and watch as one of their neighbors was gunned down in the street, she reluctantly agreed. She also agreed to pick up some food and supplies for the shop kitchen.

Satisfied with his solution to the problem and Jimmy's offer to help all Ezee had to do now was to convince DJ to trust a cop. He hoped the last nights gunfire scared him enough to realize how deadly serious his situation was. Someone was trying to kill him, and they almost succeeded.

"Dude you need to get this through your head, those gang bangers are not playing. They aren't trying to scare you they are going to kill you! They kill people for wearing the wrong color shirt, don't think they'll ever stop coming for you. They don't even quit if they're in the hospital, in jail and they would even haunt you from the grave until you jumped off a bridge. They must be stopped!"

"I suppose I don't have much of a choice." DJ conceded.

It was decided that working at the accounting firm was too risky. DJ called his boss and requested a week's leave of absence. His boss knew he was having marital issues and assumed this was the reason. DJ let him think that.

He would need to keep working at the casino. It was risky and he would need a plan to keep himself safe. His bills still had to be paid. For the duration he would get rides to and from the office.

Only three people would know where he was staying, Jimmy, Ezee and Maria. No exceptions. The detective investigating the latest shooting would only know that he was in hiding, not were.

Jimmy dragged a cot down from his attic and brought it to the shop. He cleared out a corner in what was used as a changing room. He hadn't been that busy lately, so he wasn't worried about anyone wondering why a man was sleeping in the building.

He unpacked the groceries Maria sent with him.

Still questioning what the hell he was thinking, he set up a T.V. on one of the kitchen islands.

Ezee walked in with DJ and the three men shook hands.

Jimmy showed DJ around and told him he had to get home. "Lock the door behind me and don't open for anyone or anything. I'll always call you and say I'm standing on the other side of it. If I don't call first, don't open the door.

The three decided that DJ would not get another rental car. He would alternate driving Jimmy's old Jeep and being chauffeured by Ezee or Jimmy.

DJ agreed and the three men said goodnight.

After drinking a beer, and eating some chips, DJ passed out on the cot. He slept better than he had in at least a week.

Jimmy called at 8:45 a.m. Luckily DJ heard his phone ring. He'd been sound asleep. Jimmy brought coffee and breakfast sandwiches. "This may not be so bad." DJ thought.

The two of them chatted on and off throughout the morning, mostly about cabinet building and running a business. More serious conversation started after lunch.

"What does DJ stand for?" Jimmy asked. "I'd rather not say." DJ mumbled. "How about this then," Jimmy started, "From what Ezee told me, except for this nonsense with your wife you haven't been in trouble with the law since you were a kid, you're a straight guy so why the hell do you hate cops so much?"

"They profile my people. That's a fact. Cops shoot Black people for no reason other than the color of their skin." "I can't argue with you about the profiling, DJ it happens, but if I stop a car with 5 or 6 Black youths driving around the same project for about an hour at 3am we both know they are not car-pooling to work. There are without any doubt bad cops out there. There's also bad priests, bad teachers, bad parents, and the list goes on and on. I honestly don't believe it has everything to do with skin color. The profiling is wrong too but statistically it makes sense, sadly. Like stop and frisk. No one thinks it's right, but it takes a lot of illegal guns off the street. The innocent people shot by cops are rare. I get it, one is too many. You need to know not all cops are good people but 99.9% of us are. It would be so much more productive to work together. Cops have a right to be safe too. I promise you the good cops hate the bad cops as much as you do."

DJ felt himself getting aggravated and Jimmy noticed the change in his demeanor. "We don't have to agree on everything, but we can both agree that keeping you safe is the most important thing we can do right now." Jimmy patted DJ on the back. "Let's put you to work so you don't go out of your mind with boredom all day."

The two men agreed to disagree, and they worked side by side during the day for a week. Their conversations got deeper, and they started to understand and respect one another's opinions and beliefs.

Jimmy tried to convince his new friend that he should report his wife and kids missing. "Have you considered she could have been taken against her will?" Of course, DJ wished it were against her will, but he knew she did this to hurt him, and he had no desire to save her. What was hurting him, tearing his heart apart the most was that his kids were being used in the process. He had no choice but to believe she wouldn't hurt them.

~

Jimmy was able to tug on a few loose threads to get some valuable intel from his tenant. He passed on Magda's address and the first name of her boyfriend as well as the first name of Deasia's boyfriend. DJ also gave him decent descriptions of the three men that he saw outside the casino and of the man who was in the passenger seat shooting at him in front of his house. The police already had a good description of the Camaro, which was nowhere to be found.

DJ asked Jimmy to convince his buddies that the Camaro was the same car, and the shooter was the same shooter that attacked him on the Expressway.

Careful not to let his new friend know that he was sharing certain personal information he took his time gaining DJ's trust.

The cabinet business wasn't lighting the world on fire, but Jimmy was able to give DJ some work to do, and he spent his mornings teaching DJ a few carpentry skills. It turned out he had some talent, and he was enjoying his newly discovered hobby. He was grateful Jimmy was able to pay him a few bucks for keeping the showroom clean.

It was Friday and everyone in the shop was working on pumping out a huge order that was due to be delivered the following week. DJ couldn't understand why they were working so hard, why they were determined to finish it when it wasn't due to be delivered until Tuesday.

He was hoping to get out early and meet up with Ezee to drink a few beers by the bay.

As he was sweeping up saw dust he couldn't help noticing Hector, one of the carpenters motioning what looked like a gang signal to Jose another one of the carpenters. It was the okay sign, the one made by holding the thumb and fore finger in in the shape of an "o" and the other three fingers instead of facing up, were pointing across the body.

This unnerved DJ to say the least. Were they gang bangers? Were these guys ratting him out? When he saw Luxy, one of the salesgirl's walks into the showroom flashing the same sign and yelling, "Boss man says ten-minutes everyone," He grabbed her and asked what was going on. "You mean zero-three?" She laughed, "You come with me, and I'll take you. It's the best thing about being part of Jimmy's crew."

Once all the tools were put away and the last of the cabinets were wrapped for delivery everyone headed to the front of the showroom where Jimmy was handing out envelopes containing paychecks.

Victor, another employee said, "Man, I got more people hating me now because I mentioned your name Jimmy." "What's so different about this time Vic?" Jimmy asked with a hint of sarcasm. The six-foot-three man was fuming. "This cat doesn't even know you, but I hear him throwing around your name. I listened at first and then he says that dude Jimmy stole some poor old woman's house. I couldn't keep my mouth shut then. I says to him, are you sure you got the right dude? I know the man. I work for him and never seen him take anything from anyone let alone a house. The guy gets nastier with me, so I have no choice but to get up in his face. I told him, you know me, and you know I don't lie and I'm telling you that guy don't hurt people. He helps people!" Hector jumps in and says, "You better ask Jose about that." He laughed as Jimmy handed him his paycheck and Victor pushed him towards the door. Victor continues, "So I told this clown you know I don't lie and if you keep bad mouthing people saying they did shit you didn't witness; you are going to have a huge problem with me." Jimmy said, "Little bro don't get involved with the haters. If this clown chooses to believe that negative bullshit without even trying to find out if it's true or even trying to meet me, that's his loss and one more person I don't need to know. He's an idiot. I didn't steal anyone's house, so you all know. The house across the street from me was a drug house. It wasn't being kept up and there was trash all over including the people in and out all day and night. An older woman owned the place. She inherited it but she lives in another state. I bought the house from her, took the mess off her hands."

Victor shook his head. "Like I said, you help people. It's all wrong for people to go around talking smack. And quit calling me little bro Jimmy. I ain't little and its bad enough people already think we are brothers." "Sorry man," Jimmy laughed, "I know you don't drink but are you coming to eat?" Looking disappointed Vic shook his head, "No man my mom is making a special dinner tonight. She has company coming and I promised to be there."

Luxy grabbed her check from Jimmy's hand and said, "I sure do drink and eat and if you all can't keep up, I'll bring DJ back later." Jimmy laughed, "I know you can drink my ass under the table and I'm not even trying to keep up with you babe."

DJ grabbed his check and jumped into Luxy's big old Lincoln. "Girl why does Jimmy hire all these rough dudes?" She laughed, "Because he can tell that deep down they are good people that made mistakes. Most of them work darn hard to prove how good they are and to prove they won't fuck up again if they're given a chance." DJ looked over at Luxy particularly the artwork covering her right arm. He had wanted to get a tattoo but hadn't thought about it lately. "What screw up did you commit?" He asked her. "Nothing bitch! Just because I'm Spanish, you assume I done some crime. Guess what? In fact, I have my doctorate degree in business management. Why do you think Jimmy is so busy?"

Admittedly a bit taken back DJ smiled and asked, "How did he find you?" Victor and I grew up together, our families are close. He got caught up in some big drug deal gone wrong and ended up doing federal time. No one would hire him with that record, so I asked Ezee to give him a chance. Those two bumped heads constantly, but he is a good worker, so Ezee asked Jimmy to give him a chance. Vic has been with Jimmy since day one. Once he started getting busy, he was having trouble with all the paperwork and office stuff. Victor told him he knew someone that might be able to straighten things out. I met him and could at once tell he was good people, and I also knew I would enjoy the challenge of growing his business. Seeing how Jimmy is a good person and honestly wants to leave people better off than when he found them, or they found him is sappy, but I admire him for all of it.

DJ could see that Jimmy put up a good guy front, but all cops are creepy to some degree. Some are even thugs. He remembered what Hector said about Jose thinking Jimmy wasn't a nice guy, that he didn't want to help him. "What about Jose? He doesn't buy Jimmy's good guy act does he?" Luxy started laughing hard. DJ worried about her driving; she was laughing so hard. Once she got it together she said, "Jose came in looking for work because the word is out there in town that Jimmy will hire you even if you were locked up as long as you do your job and stay clean. A month or so after he started Jose asked Jimmy if he remembered him. It wasn't the first time one of the guys approached him with that question. It's a small town and in some cases Jimmy was the one who locked them up. Jimmy told Jose he didn't remember him, which incensed Jose. Are you sure? He kept asking. Jimmy asked him, did I lock you up? Why don't you tell me what happened, I honestly don't remember you or what happened that has you so agitated. Jose continued to get angrier. You kicked my ass Jose finally blurted out. Jimmy looked at Jose and still couldn't place him. Look he said to Jose, in my job I had to kick a lot of asses. It's unfortunate but that's the way it is sometimes. Seeing that Jose desperately needed a resolution, Jimmy said to him, look I don't remember that situation because I was only doing my job. It wasn't because of any hate or ill will towards you or anyone, again I was only doing my job. God doesn't let me be bothered with those memories, I'm lucky that way. Jose was taken a bit back by Jimmy's explanation, but he was still pissed off that Jimmy didn't remember something that got him locked up for three to five years. He started screaming at Jimmy, in the shop in front of everyone. But you didn't have to kick my ass like that!" DJ said, "That must have been awkward for everyone.

"To say the least," Luxy continued, "Jimmy calmly said to Jose let me see, you did some crime, so I was called. You were mad because I told you what the law required me to do. Then not liking what I was telling you, you threatened me, and I told you if you didn't comply things were going to get much worse for you. Jose nodded smugly and his shoulders slumped. Jimmy continued to tell him, "I know you're mad and don't like your choices but fighting me is only going to get your ass kicked, and more charges brought against you. I gave you every chance, I know I did because that is what I always did before I kicked someone's ass for not complying. Fighting me was not going to change your circumstance it was only going to make things worse, and I made that perfectly clear to you. I did to everyone. Never did I treat anyone in a way I wouldn't want my own family member to be treated by a cop. Jose slumped down even further and told Jimmy he was right, and it was his own fault for not listening. Jimmy told Jose he thought he was a good guy, much better than some of the other clowns he locked up and he hoped he would stay. That was that but now every once in a while some smart ass brings it up."

Luxy pulled her Lincoln into a reserved parking spot and said, "We're here." DJ completely forgot to ask where they were going but now that they were here there was no need.

It was a popular Chinese restaurant. There was a line at the door, but Luxy pulled DJ along behind her and made her way past the hostess, smiling of course, towards the back room. There was a rectangular shaped table so large it jutted into the dining room. There were also several round tables in the room. Jimmy recognized several politicians seated at one and two community leaders seated at another. Already seated at their table was a few coworkers. There was no sign of Jimmy, yet.

Jimmy liked to make a grand entrance. He parked his car in the alley, entered through the back door and walked through the kitchen. Walking through this bustling kitchen brought back memories of his family's waterfront restaurant in Philadelphia. He loved working there, but he also dreamed of being a police officer. Now he dreamed of one day bringing a restaurant like that to the waterfront in Atlantic City. He also envisioned adding an entertainment complex.

He was growing tired of being stuck in the warehouse for long hours with no windows. He longed for the old days of crowds and constant excitement.

Until then he was able to replicate that here at his oasis. The owner who also did the cooking himself loved Jimmy because his Friday night get togethers, with his crew created such a buzz and in the restaurant business buzz is everything. People now waited in lines to get in on Friday and Saturday nights if they wanted to sit in the main dining room. They enjoyed listening to the commotion coming from the back room, knowing there was a strong possibility that there were celebrities enjoying a meal there.

Jimmy stopped in the kitchen to give the chef instructions for the special order for him and his guests. Not much of what he ordered was listed on the menu. He opened a large bag he was carrying and placed several bottles of wine on the counter. This wasn't just any wine, it was Jimmy's homemade wine. He made several types, but his specialty a sweet, dry wine that was reserved only for Maria.

He stood by the kitchen door where he could see his table but those seated couldn't see him. Taking a few minutes to eves drop on his employees he waited for the topic of their conversation to change. When they mentioned his wine, he made his grand entrance with a waiter in tow, who started putting glasses of one of Jimmy's sweet wines in front each guest. Everyone cheered not necessarily because

Jimmy was there but because his alcohol was there. This batch was sweet but not too sugary. Jimmy never added chemicals to kill the yeast, so it was strong but not overbearing. You would never know how strong it was by the taste, it was mild and flavorful but after the first glass, there was a noticeable buzz.

After stuffing themselves with the delicious meal Jimmy chose for them, and most of the wine was gone, Hector said, "Hey Jimmy if DJ is going to work with us shouldn't we take him camping first?" Everyone laughed and jeered in agreement. DJ instantly felt uncomfortable, even scared. Did they want to see him dead too? Feeling the wine, he said, "Woah you'll. Enough alright!" "Relax DJ it's only tradition. Once a year we go on a camping trip together," Luxy explained, "It's a bonding exercise for all of us." Jimmy continued, "Let me ask you DJ, what if we were camping and eating and drinking like this; but drinking much more because no one would have to drive, and you passed out. When you woke up the next morning with the sun bright and burning your eyes, your head pounding and suddenly you realize your butt naked and you know something happened against your will, would you tell anyone?"

DJ looked around the table at each one of them. He was disgusted by their smirks. "You all are some nasty people. Really nasty people." He said realizing he was the butt of a sick joke, "I'd fuck up the one who did it, no doubt!" "But would you tell anyone," Luxy asked trying to be serious. "No." DJ answered. "You wanna go camping?" Jimmy asked. "Fuck you. Fuck you all!" DJ answered.

"Lighten up DJ" Jimmy said, "It's only a sick joke. You're right it's all disgusting." Here have some more wine."

DJ held his glass out and as Jimmy poured the wine he said, "Remember I know where you all sleep." Everyone laughed even harder.

As Luxy drove DJ back to the shop she could tell he was still upset. "Don't be mad about that stupid joke," She said, "They do that to everyone. "But did they say that to you? Did Jimmy speak to you that way?" "You guys all get so upset by that. It's a bit phobic if you ask me. And yes, they did ask me, and I said, I haven't told anyone yet, why would I ever start now? I told them, I can out drink every single one of you clowns so if you were stupid drunk pawing your way to me, I would wreck you and then tell."

DJ believed her. She said, "It was worth the stupid look on their faces. Seriously though, DJ you do need to lighten up. Not everyone is out to get you. I'll see you Monday." She said as he got out of her car. She waited until he got into his car. When she drove safely away DJ got out of his car and went inside the warehouse.

DJ's head was spinning. "I work with some crazy ass people here. Camping! They are out of their minds."

He tossed and turned on the cot for at least an hour but when he finally fell asleep, he slept soundly and woke up well rested. He had no hangover symptoms. Jimmy said he wouldn't because he didn't use chemicals in his wine unlike most of the store brought brands.

"I've never been much of a wine drinker. Yours is good, I may become a wino. And no hangover, what a plus!" DJ said as Jimmy handed him a coffee from Seven-Eleven.

They talked about the IRS scam, but DJ never let on to Jimmy that he wasn't letting it go. He wasn't sure if it was because he felt stupid, or because Jimmy might think he was stupid.

Barely a week passed before Ezee started hearing from several sources, that questions were being asked about DJ's whereabouts. While it was comforting to know the gang had no idea where he was it reminded the three of them not let their guard down.

Smuggling DJ to his job at the casino was getting harder to pull off without bringing more people into their circle, and Jimmy knew that would be disastrous. They continued to come up with creative ideas to get him back and forth safely.

DJ continued to get ridiculous amounts of notifications from the credit protection company. He spotted an ad for a service that supplied protection for your information from over sea's thieves and scammers. DJ remembering the fake agent that called him had an Indian ascent, signed up for the service.

While bored at work one night he scrolled through them for the hell of it. One notification was from the over sea's service. It caught his eye, and he couldn't stop thinking about it. The notification said there was a bank in an African town he never heard of that was holding money for him. $5,000,000 to be exact. Stunned, his mind started racing.

Half- jokingly he called Berch and told him about the notification. Berch had a few opinions but the one that was tempting DJ was the idea that he should hop on a plane and get his money! As ridiculous as the idea was, it also made perfect sense.

He couldn't stop thinking about it.

As much as he wanted to confide in Jimmy, he decided not to. He didn't want his new friend to think he completely lost his mind. Secretly though, DJ was trying to hatch a plan.

He had nothing to lose.

Secretly planning for the possibility that the location of the safe house could be breached Jimmy strategically placed a few weapons around the warehouse. He taped two Beretta pistols to the top of the inside of the center island in the showroom. In an umbrella stand by the side door he put a wooden baseball bat. It wasn't easy but in the rafters he strategically placed twelve bricks that could be dropped down on MS13 heads, if needed.

All he told DJ was if someone gets in, get up to the rafters and hide.

Chapter 10:

The Boss

It's hard to explain the knot you feel in your gut when you enter a courtroom.

They're always so dark and it isn't only the brown paneling on the walls. DJ had no choice but to trust the short, pudgy public defender. He was relieved to see he was already there.

"Make sure your phone is off," The attorney said without even looking at DJ "He doesn't care about me at all." DJ thought to himself.

He was relieved when he turned to see his mom, Ezee, and Jimmy sitting in the row behind him. Then he looked up and felt nauseous as a female judge paraded across the front of the courtroom and took her seat on the throne of judgement.

There were no signs of any gang members or Deasia. DJ was disappointed. As ridiculous as it was, he missed her. Thoughts of his kids that went from the happiest memories to the most intense worry he ever felt made it so hard to concentrate on anything. "What if they aren't okay?"

He wondered if the trial could be continued to a later date because she didn't appear.

The judge questioned Deasia's attorney and when he informed her that he had no idea where his client was, the judge dismissed the entire case and the Domestic Violence Restraining order.

Jimmy's suggestion to demand a trial worked perfectly. "That cop ain't half bad," DJ mumbled. He was relieved, but Deasia and his kids were still missing and with each day that passed the more he wondered if he'd ever see them again.

The word on the street was MS13 was still relentlessly looking for him so the three of them decided he should stay hunkered down at the warehouse and all precautions were still in place.

Gang members were taking turns parking across the street from DJ's house. It appeared they were taking shifts. Taking Jimmy's advice Ezee and other neighbors reported the strange vehicle parked on his block and that the occupants of the car were blaring music at all hours of the day and night. The calls resulted in a patrol- cars driving by and shining their light on the car. The driver would pull away only to pull back up in the area a short time later.

He was still getting hundreds of notifications each day from the credit protection agency. His friends and even his divorce attorney felt like he needed to find a way to scam the scammers.

The original notification he received from the international fraud alert company saying an account was opened using his identity, in Africa was hard to forget. $5,000,000 American dollars.

It was like a joke to everyone else, but he couldn't stop seriously thinking and fantasizing about all that money.

Taking a chance, he decided to speak with his boss Levi Ziman. Levi is an elderly Russian Jew, and the smartest businessperson DJ knew.

Levi came to the United States as a young man to attend college, majoring in business. He started a small accounting firm in New York. Once his kids grew up he and his wife moved to Atlantic City. The couple opened a financial advising firm in a storefront.

DJ started working for them in high school. He cleaned the office, went to the post office and he picked up coffee and bagels.

There were never any clients in the office, Levi did all his business on the phone or online. The couple often travelled to Israel, the middle east and sometimes even Russia. At one time DJ wondered and even imagined them as spies.

Whatever he was doing business wise back then didn't matter because DJ couldn't think of anyone smarter when it came to money and banking. He had to trust someone, and he knew Levi wouldn't make jokes or make fun of him. He gave the old guy a call.

To DJ's surprise, Levi agreed to investigate the validity of the account.

Lying on his cot at the warehouse DJ remembered Levi smoking cigars. He could balance one on his lips and inhale without holding it while talking. DJ could almost see and smell the smoke and hear him yelling, "Go down to the corner store and get me a pack of Garcia Vega Elegantes!"

He grinned. Those were the days.

The next day Levi informed DJ that the account in Africa was indeed authentic, and he suggested strongly that DJ get on a plane, quickly and retrieve his money. He offered to fund the trip for a percentage of the cash recovered. DJ was stunned.

"I'll get everything in order. It'll take a couple of days. We'll need to get you a passport and I'll get the soft currency exchanges set up for you. These will help you get the cash into the United States like Western Union but without paying taxes and without having to explain to the government where the money came from. Because this is such a large amount of money, it will take quite a few businesses to handle the transfers. I've used them myself. I'm going to the airport to buy a plane ticket for you from JFK to Lago's, Africa."

DJ's adrenalin was off the charts. "This IS happening!" He was excited and at the same time a bit terrified. What he didn't think about was who put $5,000,000 in an account using his name and what the consequences might be for withdrawing that money from the account.

All he could think about was getting his kids back and supplying a fabulous life for them. He thought about starting his own business, something that would enable him to buy a bigger, better house on a much better block. And of course, he would be doing something special for his mother.

Of course, Levi knew that the odds were not in DJ's favor, and he would never make it out of Africa alive. His hope was that he would at least make it to the businesses and complete the money transfers. If he got that far Levi would be able to send someone to collect the cash for himself. The old man couldn't help himself, his greed ruled him, always.

He chose not to tell his new cop friend or Ezee about the notifications, the money, or the trip. Instead, he told him an elderly relative in California died recently and an attorney let him know that he may have left him something in his will. He hoped once Jimmy realized he was gone he would assume he'd gone to California to collect his inheritance.

The details were vague, so Jimmy at once knew it was a bunch of lies. The guy was growing on him but whatever he was up to had nothing to do with him, so he shook it off.

Travelling was not something DJ ever did. He was never on a plane and the furthest he'd travelled was on I-95 South to Virginia to buy fireworks.

Levi bought DJ's airline ticket and told him he would have his passport, and travel documents ready soon. He couldn't help but grin when the old guy told him he could pick his ticket up at the counter in the airport the morning of his flight.

Luckily, he had a backpack and a suitcase with him in the warehouse. Now he needed to decide what to pack. Levi was going to drop him off at the airport so there was no need to worry about a ride.

~

Jimmy continued to pass information over to his Atlantic City Police Department friends who in turn reported to other organizations. All of them were under the assumption that eventually a hitman would make an attempt on DJ's life.

Against DJ's wishes Jimmy also shared with them that Deasia and the kids were missing. They were able to trace her to Texas, but they needed DJ to file kidnapping charges against her. If Jimmy could at least get him to report her missing they could get the FBI involved officially. Until then they would do their best to keep eyes on her and the kids.

Maria dropped DJ off at work. The entire ride to the casino he thanked her for the meals she provided, the rides and for letting him stay in the warehouse. Originally against the arrangement he was growing on her.

He was so preoccupied thinking about his secret trip and what he was going to do with all that money he almost missed the Camaro that drove slowly down the street and was pulling up in front of the casino. Out of the corner of his eye he watched as the passenger side window rolled down, slowly. DJ ran to the side of the building. Through the landscaping he could see the car moving slowly along the curb. He watched as the passenger got out and walked towards the boardwalk and the back of the building. Once he could no longer see him DJ darted for the front door, entered the code, and let himself in.

"What's wrong with you?" The guard he was relieving yelled.. "Nothing. I didn't want to be late, so I was rushing." He walked towards the back of the casino praying that all the doors were already locked and bolted. Taking a deep breath, he carefully checked each one and then he consciously stayed away from the large windows that made up three sides of the massive first floor.

He made his way to an office on the second floor that had smaller windows but gave him a good view of all three sides of the exterior of the building.

Convinced that they drove off he sat down at one of the desks and texted Jimmy to let him know what happened.

Jimmy said both he and Ezee would pick him up in a different car and they'd take the long way back to the warehouse. He suggested it was time for DJ to tell his boss he needed a leave of absence for personal reasons.

DJ was planning to do that anyway. He was leaving for Africa in two days!

His boss wasn't happy and said he couldn't guarantee his job would be there when he returned. He did wish DJ luck though.

Still stuck in the office for a few hours and bored he called Berch. Teasing he said "You're gonna go get that money aren't you?" DJ laughed and said, "Yeah right."

He shook hands with his relief and slipped out the front door. Ezee pulled up as close to the curb as possible and DJ slipped into the back seat of an old Ford Escort. "Where did you get this thing?" DJ laughed. "It belongs to my aunt." He laughed and Ezee handed him a beer.

Ezee drove North through Brigantine on back roads and then back to Atlantic City using main roads. He made U-turns and went around the block several times until he was 100% positive no one was following them.

Relieved when DJ told him he sort of quit his job, Ezee said, "I know it's gonna be rough financially for a while. Let's hope Jimmy and his cop friends can get to the bottom of it sooner than later. The stress of getting him back and forth to work was taking a toll on everyone involved.

Once DJ was sure Jimmy was gone for the night, he texted Levi. The old man brought along two cigars and a six pack. He also brought $5000 in cash. Looking at the cash on the granite counter made what was about to happen real.

The two sat there reminiscing over old stories. DJ smoked his first cigar ever and realized it wasn't as cool as he thought it would be, way back then. Levi still balanced the stogie on his lips and DJ was still fascinated.

His old friend did his best to explain the process of how businesses wire cash back to the states using other businesses. Finally, he was starting to understand how it worked and it made sense.

Together they packed DJ's carryon bag and his backpack. Levi instructed him on how to answer certain questions that customs agents might ask.

They decided to put both bags in the trunk of Levi's old Cadillac then to ensure a quicker getaway in the morning. Levi would return the next night at 5:45 to get DJ to the airport for his 11:00 p.m. flight to Africa.

Sleep didn't come easy that night. How would he ever work all day with Jimmy, without saying a word about leaving? He wondered what flying would be like and he wondered if he'd see any elephants or lions in Africa. Trying to focus more on having $5,000,000 to come home to he closed his eyes and imagined how his life could change.

Jimmy was busy all day so it was easier than DJ thought it would be to keep his secret. "Want me to bring you some dinner back?" Jimmy asked as he got ready to call it a day. It was 4:30. "No I have plenty of stuff in the fridge," DJ answered, "I don't want to waste the leftovers in there." "Suit yourself then." Jimmy said as he left.

Once the door to the shop was closed and locked DJ was filled with anxiety. He made himself a sandwich and finished the last beer in the refrigerator. He took a quick shower and put on a track suit and his brand- new retro Jordan's.

His phone vibrated on the counter. Levi was outside.

He took a deep breath and opened the shop door. Immediately he caught a glimpse of that damned Camaro parked on the other side of the street, three blocks down. He jumped into the Caddy and told Levi to step on it. "We got no time to mess with this," DJ shouted.

The old guy had some impressive driving skills. There was no sign of the Camaro. They took Atlantic Avenue towards Virginia and then turned left onto North, North Carolina Avenue. Still no sign of the gang banger. Without using a blinker Levi turned left onto Baltic Avenue and used the right lane to merge onto the Atlantic City Expressway.

There were still remnants of rush hour traffic, but it didn't slow them down. Conversation was so fluid and so relaxing that DJ couldn't believe it when he looked up and saw signs for the Belt Parkway.

Levi gave his prodigy a few last- minute instructions, hugged him. and said, "It's time for these mother fuckers to get stung!" DJ thanked his old friend and walked through the automatic doors into unfamiliar territory.

He quickly found the ticket counter and chose the line with the prettiest agent behind the counter. She was friendly which helped calm DJ's nerves. She gave him instructions on how to navigate his way through security, customs, and how to find his gate.

The waiting area was full of travelers, but he found a seat next to an elderly gentleman. They exchanged pleasantries. He scanned the crowd looking for anyone that looked like they might want to kill him.

With his nerves getting the best of him he walked over to a kiosk and bought a large bottle of water, an apple, and a bag of chips.

When the gate agent called his row to board, he panicked. "What the hell am I doing?" He wanted to turn and run but instead he kept walking forward. Halfway down the jetway it got cold. Keeping his head down he stepped onto the plane. When he looked up he saw the prettiest smile. The flight attendant, captain and copilot welcomed him on board and directed him to go through first class and told him he would find his seat on the right side of the airplane.

He placed his carry on into the overhead compartment and slid his backpack under the seat in front of his. He took a deep breath and slid open the window shade.

Chapter 11:
The Trip

Sitting back in the seat, he buckled the lap belt, and took a deep breath. When Levi bought his ticket, he thought the window seat would be the best choice. DJ wasn't so sure. He started feeling claustrophobic.

If he could've bought the ticket online himself like a *normal* person there would have been time to think it through but that was out of the question in this case.

He'd never been on an airplane before. In his wildest dreams, which were the only times he ever even imagined taking any sort of a trip or a vacation, Deasia would be sitting by his side. She'd be wearing a pretty dress, that Lilly designer stuff she liked so much, and he'd be buying her those stupid umbrella drinks one after another.

"I'm sitting on a plane and I'm flying to Africa," He whispered to himself, "Crazy! Why didn't I think to bring someone with me?" He shook that idea off because there wasn't anyone he could trust, not with this.

An older woman sat in the middle seat next to him and a middle-aged woman took the aisle seat. He felt relieved and hoped his profuse sweating would stop before it scared them.

Not aware that the loud thump he heard was the door to the plane being pulled shut and secured by a crew member, he jumped. The woman next to him patted his wrist. "Is this your first flight dear?" "It's that obvious huh," DJ laughed. "Relax and focus on something positive." She suggested.

The plane jerked forward. Normally DJ wasn't the praying type, but this seemed like the perfect time to start. He folded his hands in his lap, bowed his head asked God to protect him on his long journey.

They sat on the runway for what seemed like forever. Finally, they started rolling again, slowly at first and then faster. "Here we go," the lady said patting his wrist again, "It's okay just breathe," she said softly, "once we get up in the air it will seem like we're not moving at all."

Feeling dizzy DJ closed his eyes and thanked God for putting this kind, calming woman next to him.

The three of them had drinks, talked for hours, and napped. It's amazing what you can learn about someone during a 13-hour flight. DJ told them he was on a mission to claim an inheritance. He didn't feel too bad because it was a half -truth.

He told them about his three children and that his wife, whom he loved with all his heart left him for another man, a gang member. Not any old gang, an MS13 gang member!

His new friends expressed their horror and insisted he do whatever he had to do to get his children away from those monsters and to do whatever he had to do to get custody of them. He assured the ladies he and his attorney were formulating a plan.

Both women told him they would be traveling to an impoverished area in Nigeria to do missionary work. The middle-aged woman was an infectious disease doctor, and the older woman was on sabbatical from her teaching job at a Christian school in Connecticut. Bringing God to people who desperately needed him was something she'd been wanting to do since she was a teenager. Both said this trip was a dream come true for them.

As the wheels hit the runway, DJ said a prayer of gratitude. For a first flight, this was a long one. It was also a huge check off the bucket list.

The three travelers exchanged contact information with each other. DJ was nervous at first but gave them the number to a burner phone he bought at the airport in New York. They hugged in the terminal and headed towards the customs cattle shoot.

English is a common language in Nigeria, so he was able to read most of the signs. One nearly stopped him in his tracks:

Money Laundering in Nigeria is a crime. If you are carrying cash exceeding $5,000, you will be prosecuted.

"How my gonna get out of here with any cash?" His heart sank. Wondering if they would count out the $4800 in cash he now had in his socks, wallet, and carry- on bag thanks to his boss. He started to sweat again. Doubting if he even counted the cash correctly he started pacing in his place in line. He looked around at the others in the long lines and realized he wasn't the only one sweating.

Striking up a conversation with several other American men on basketball and football helped pass the time and settled his nerves.

The line was moving quickly. As he approached customs an officer asked him the purpose of his trip. He tried to remain calm, which was impossible. He never saw so many guns being carried out in the open.

He responded the way his boss coached him. "I'm in the country for pleasure."

The customs officer smirked knowing full well there was no way this guy was in Africa for pleasure. He called over to some other guards and in their native language said, "Look at this guy. He's going to be kidnapped for ransom or he's going to be hunting big game in the country next door."

DJ had no idea what they were saying. More armed guards approached. A large bang sounded behind him. DJ swung around without thinking. The customs official had stamped his passport, loudly. "Enjoy your stay." The official said as he handed DJ his passport. As he walked away he heard them laughing. Fighting the urge to turn and look at them he kept walking forward.

The airport lobby was a mix a modern art and old graffiti. It was hard to tell if the bullet holes were modern or antique.

He stood back on the sidewalk to see how one got the attention of cab drivers in this country. Feeling victorious after surviving customs, he was confident he could find his way to the bank that had *his* stolen money.

The cab driver assured DJ he knew that bank.

As they pulled up to the one- story brick building the first thing DJ noticed was the thick bars on the door and the windows.

DJ asked the driver to wait, and the man agreed.

As he entered the bank four heavily armed security guards greeted him. "What is your business here?" One asked as he stood inches from DJ "I'm here to close my account." The guard demanded ID and an account number.

He took the papers from DJ including his passport and walked behind a counter. After searching through a large ledger, the guard walked to a podium that stood in the middle of the lobby and placed a phone call. He walked back towards DJ and said, "Follow me." The guard pushed some numbers on a security pad and then pulled open a large metal door that led to what looked like a small waiting room. "Have a seat." The guard said before handing DJ back his papers. Then he turned and went back through the metal door to the lobby.

The small room had six chairs. Three on one side and three on the other with two large square tables in the middle. DJ looked for a magazine. There were none. One wall was full of soccer posters, and another had an I-Phone and several banking posters. There were no windows.

Ten minutes later a large man, he had to be at least seven- foot tall, approached DJ and extended his hand. The two shook hands and then the man invited DJ to follow him down a narrow hallway to his office.

The man told DJ to take a seat and he walked away. He returned with two cups of tea, placing one in front of DJ, and then taking a seat behind his large mahogany desk.

After looking at a computer screen for a few minutes the bank manager realized the size of the withdraw DJ was requesting.

"Are you unhappy with the service of our bank?" The man asked. Thinking for a minute before answering, DJ replied, "No I'm not unhappy. I want to have my money closer to home. It'll be easier if a business opportunity presents itself." "We can authorize business anywhere in the world." The banker suggested. "Yes, I understand," DJ said, "But some opportunities require cash." "Oh, I see." The banker responded.

"Did you bring the account numbers of the businesses you'd like the money transferred to over the next year?"

The question caught DJ completely off guard. A year? He took deep breaths.

"It's my money," DJ started, "Why can't I get it and go? I'm in a hurry."

"Yes, you are correct, but this large amount of cash is not here, in this building. The most I could gather is about $800,000 U.S. dollars, and even that amount will take some time." "How long?" "About eight months the banker replied. This is a poor country, but I can give you credit to stay at a hotel and, also to eat for the duration of your stay."

Remembering the list of companies his boss gave him, that would be able to wire the money to businesses in New Jersey for him because he wouldn't be able to fly out of this country with more than $5000 in cash, he took it from his pocket and handed it to the banker. "Could you possibly give these companies a letter of credit and allow them to wire the money to me in the States and when you have the cash together, you can reimburse them?"

The banker, realizing what DJ was doing said he could arrange the letters of credit and he'd be willing to send $800,000 per year. "You will need to return each year to deliver the new letters of credit to the businesses. They change frequently," He continued, "But this list of businesses is *no* good. These are Jewish companies. This is a Muslim country. Our banks are barred from dealing with any Jewish businesses."

"That's racist." DJ said. "It is what it is." The banker replied.

The banker took a notebook from his top desk drawer and jotted down the names and addresses of four Muslim businesses that would take a letter of credit and be willing to transfer the money for him. He handed the list to DJ and made a phone call, speaking in the native language.

A few minutes later, two guards entered the office one of them carrying a backpack.

The banker explained to DJ there was $50,000 in the bag. "Return tomorrow morning. I'll have the credit slips for you, minus the banks percentage for making arrangements with the Muslim businesses for you."

Lagos was much more modern than he imagined it would be. Relieved that his cab driver pulled up to a hotel that looked like an actual hotel, he offered him a larger tip than he read was custom. In turn the driver handed DJ his business card and said he was at his service during his stay.

"What's your name man?" "Chukwuemeka" the driver answered. "Whoa," DJ said, not sure he would ever be able to repeat that. "Can I call you Chuks?" "Yes, yes!" The two shook hands. DJ showed the driver the piece of paper the bank manager gave him with the list of Muslim businesses. "Can you take me to them?" DJ asked. Chuks stared down at the addresses and seemed to take forever to answer.

"This is quite a long journey. I need to let my family know. Get rest and I'll return for you in the morning.

With $55,000 burning a huge hole in his pocket, DJ walked up to the counter in the hotel lobby. He requested a suite with a balcony. The clerk stopped shuffling papers and said,

"361,500.00 Naira." Panicked at the thought of how expensive that sounded, DJ stuttered and asked the clerk if he could give her a deposit in American currency and pay the balance after a business meeting. She smiled and said, "That will be sixty dollars per night, American please sir." They both laughed.

Memories of what happened over the last few months and how he ended up here, and why he was in this terrifying and at the same time adrenaline inducing situation flashed through his mind. One comforting thought was if any MS13 douches followed him, he'd be able to spot them immediately while they would have a tough time picking him out of any crowd in this country.

Feeling safe from assassination attempts by a gang member for the first time in months, all he had to do now was to hope he could trust the bank manager and the taxi driver to get him and his money out of Africa without being caught by the military or the police and quickly before the crooks figured out what he was up to.

He opened the drapes and stepped out onto the balcony to see what kind of a view the room offered. "Not bad," he thought. It was all city but off in the distance he could see the bluest water. "I'm definitely not in AC anymore," he thought. Most of the buildings were modern but he did spot a few that seemed old, even older than old. Whenever he thought of Africa this was nothing like the picture that came to mind. Lions and giraffes came to mind. Grass huts and dusty dirt roads came to mind. Shaking his head, he went back inside, closed the drapes, and spread out on the king- sized bed, on the side closest to the door and fell sound asleep.

The phone on the nightstand between the two king sized beds rang, startling him. His driver arrived. DJ splashed some cold water on his face. A shave would have to wait. He put on a clean shirt, a tie and a suit jacket and gathered the room key, his wallet, and the papers with the information he needed to find the businesses. Before he left he put one of the backpacks holding cash in the room safe. He made his way down the hall to the elevator.

Feeling Chuks eyeballing him in the rearview mirror, DJ squirmed in the back of the cab and started shaking. "What you up to man," Chuks asked. DJ focused on not making eye contact with the driver. He didn't answer. "Come on man. You're one of those cash mules, yes?" "What's a cash mule?" DJ asked wondering if what he was doing was a thing.

"Mules deliver illegally gained funds to businesses here in this country. These towns you are traveling to are known for this type of activity." "Nah Chuks I'm not delivering any money. I'm collecting money, my own money."

Chuks grinned and nodded but knew something wasn't quite on the up and up. He already liked DJ and hoped he knew what he was doing. "Will they speak English," DJ asked. "Yes."

After safely retrieving the letters of credit from the guard at the bank, Chuks drove to his house to exchange his cab for a Toyota pick-up truck. "It will be easier to travel where we're going in this," he said smiling.

They traveled several hours to an office building that served as the sales department and call center for a furniture company and a real estate office. Both were fronts for a global money laundering network.

DJ brushed off the front of his suit. As he opened the front door of the office building he spotted a guard with a rifle on the left of the entryway and another on the right. His heart sank but he held his head high and kept walking. Straight ahead in the center of the lobby was a counter. Behind it were two men and a woman with a big bright smile. Choosing the woman, of course DJ approached her. "I'd like to take care of this," he said and handed her the piece of paper with the name of the man he was supposed to meet.

"No; no, she said, you need to take a seat and wait." As he sat waiting he tried not to make eye contact with the guys with the guns, or anyone else for that matter.

A few minutes later the woman returned and led him into a small office.

"So; Mr. Davis we've already transferred $50,000 cash to businesses in Ukraine on your behalf and on instruction from the bank manager. The other businesses on your list will be able to transfer your money directly to the United States. We're only set up to work with Ukraine."

DJ's head was spinning.

Once you finish your business with the companies in this country you need to go to Ukraine and the businesses there will give you $50,000 in cash. From there you will go to a company in California, and they will tell you where to go in New Jersey to claim the rest of your cash.

With the thought of a total of *$800,000 a year* still spinning in his head and terrified he might pass out he asked, "Could you write those directions down for me, please." DJ tried to sound confident. "Of course. Now let me gather those credit slips you'll need. You must be quick. These things must happen fast. You'll get accustomed to it."

The man and the woman left the room and DJ was physically shaking.

He started laughing, diabolically. "They think I'm one of them," He laughed again. I'm about to get away with this."

For years DJ's friends and many strangers told him he looked like Chris Rock. It was true, of course he did. Now more than ever he needed to call on his inner Rock and the actor's magnetic charm and confidence. Any sign of weakness could be dangerous, even deadly for him.

The man reentered the office with a large envelope. It held $5000 in Nigerian money. Once you get to Ukraine there are kiosks all over the city so you can exchange some of this to Ukrainian hryvnia.

Keep yourself inside the city of Kyiv. It's well populated and safer. If you wander outside those city limits it may not be safe, in fact it's most definitely not safe.

The woman with the pretty smile entered the office and handed DJ a folder. He opened it and recognized it as the typed directions he requested.

The three of them shook hands. DJ thanked them, wished them a good day and he made his way back to the truck. He pressed himself against the back of the seat and let out a scream. WOOOOOAAAHH. Chuks laughed. "All is well Mr. DJ?" "Yes, Chuks all is well at this moment. My man, I do believe they thought I was this mule you spoke of. I need to hurry and finish my business."

At a small out of the way restaurant DJ confided in his driver. He told him a wealthy relative left him a fortune and the bank wasn't cooperating with him. They were sending him on this wild goose chase. Reading the disbelief on his drivers face DJ took the biggest chance of his life and told Chuks, who seemed completely stunned upon hearing the entire truth.

Chapter 12:
Chuks

"They tell me I have five-million U.S. dollars, yet they can't give it to me."

DJ didn't leave anything out. He explained how his wife got addicted to OxyContin and then heroin after a car accident. Then she ran off with an MS13 gang member. He told him how the entire gang not only wanted to kill him, but they also tried and almost succeeded several times. "That wasn't enough though," DJ continued, "They stole my identity, and they wiped out my bank account. $5000 which was every cent I had. One of the accountants I work for suggested I sign up with a company that keeps an eye on my credit to make sure the crooks weren't doing more damage. The credit company let me know that those scumbags opened a business account in my name here in your country. I thought coming here to collect was my best bet because I'd blend in, I wouldn't stand out here. Credit cards have also been opened in my name, and now my credit is in shambles. Honestly, it was already in shambles because of my ex and her boyfriend buying stuff in my name. My jobs are in jeopardy because I've had to hideout for weeks in a warehouse owned by retired 5-0 and I haven't been able to work, can you imagine that?" Putting his head down and then lifting it back up to look Chuks in the eye he said, "I don't know where my kids are or even if they're okay."

The driver was expressionless.

"So here I am on this journey with you and I'm collecting more cash than I've ever seen in my life. Do you know how to do these things? Can I trust you to continue helping me get this business taken care of and to get me out of this country safely?"

Although only a minute passed since DJ finished talking it felt like an hour since Chuks leaned back in his chair, folded his arms, and glared at DJ

The taxi driver had been a life saver, but DJ wondered if he read him wrong and now he was about to be scammed again. He'd caught on enough to know that you don't make negative comments or criticize a Nigerian, so he had been careful not to offend him. His driver was genuine, a good man.

Right from the beginning Chuks appreciated that DJ wasn't like most foreigners that ended up in the back seat of his taxi. Most were heavy drinkers, rude and treated him as a servant. They also never had a complete address for their destination. All of that on top of the chaotic traffic and trying to find ways safely around all the congestion added to his already great stress.

The man was also responsible for supporting his seven children, the oldest nineteen and the youngest only a six-month-old infant. He had two wives. His sister and her six children lived with him too. Her husband was murdered by the terrorists during one of the country's recent uprisings.

Now this. It could be dangerous.

He was no fan of breaking the law, but he had great empathy for this sad man sitting across from him, and he did know of these things that had his American passenger entangled.

Chuks clearly understood that Lagos, the economic capitol of Nigeria, one of the largest cities in West Africa, the fifth most populated city in the world with mostly middle class and lower socio-economic residents it is also famous for pollution, overpopulation, filth, street crime and sadly he was also aware that his beloved country was also known as the world capital of financial crimes and internet and phone scams.

Because of the rampant corruption among politicians, the military, and police it's difficult for the lower class to advance.

Putting all the chaos and negativity aside, the city is formed of two distinct areas, the mainland, and the island. The weather is always warm with only two short rainy seasons. There's plenty of beauty to be found if you know where to look starting with the beaches and the parks. The clubs and entertainment in the city are top notch.

Chuks was proud to have been born here and excited for all the entrepreneurial opportunities available to those who worked hard and were willing to take risks. He was starting to wonder if this was his opportunity to take a risk. That once in a lifetime moment for him to grab or to forever wonder "what if" he had taken that risk.

"Eat," he said abruptly, startling DJ who hadn't touched his pepper soup or his stew.

He told DJ the trip would take at least 3 days of non- stop traveling.

"Mr. DJ we have no choice but to get your business taken care of and to get you out of this country and to your next destination safely. I'm going to help you because I know you will be grateful and remember your humble friend here on the other side of the world."

DJ was relieved to say the least.

As they approached the city of Ibadan, their next stop, Chuks said they would take care of business and then spend the night. They would leave at first light for the next destination.

Everything went smoother than expected. DJ handed the credit slips to a man in a phone store and in return the man gave him instructions on where to retrieve his cash in New Jersey.

Chuks pulled the truck up to a ten-foot-tall iron gate with a sign that that read enter. On the left was a similar gate with an exit sign. In the middle was a brick walkway, and a small patch of green grass bordered with lavender flowers.

DJ registered them. They decided on adjoining rooms.

The room was tiny but adequate. Looking out the window DJ spotted a woman laboring to push a large yellow cart. "This is more like the Africa, I always envisioned." He said to himself. He looked again and saw a man pushing a wheelbarrow full of trash. The man dumped it on to the sidewalk already piled high with garbage.

In the morning, the two of them had a quick breakfast and drove further inland, taking mostly back roads through the countryside. As they traveled, both revealed more personal information. Chuks explained to DJ that at times he took jobs that kept him away from home for a month to six-weeks. He went on to say that his family understands if he is gone for more than a month with no word, they should consider him dead and plan to move on and remarry.

As they approached Ilorin, DJ was in awe of the expansive gold mosques and the large modern university. This city was much larger and cleaner than the last one.

The men at this business refused to speak with DJ because he wasn't Muslim. Chuks stepped in and did all the talking. This company was a hub for trading. They supplied most of the country with fuel, water, canned goods, farm equipment, weapons, and ammunition.

Chuks spoke to the group of men in their native language. He negotiated the fees on behalf of his American friend and collected the letters he would need to pick his money up in New Jersey.

If he was being honest this situation was the most stressful thus far. Trapped in the corner of a tiny room without any idea of what the strangers on the other side of the room were discussing was terrifying.

Once they were safely back on the road, DJ asked the question he was quite sure he didn't want the answer to. "Who exactly were those men?" "That my friend depends on who is asking and why." DJ decided he was better off not knowing.

Hours later they reached the third city. Kaduna was small and filthy. "This is the dirtiest city in Nigeria," Chuks informed DJ, "It's also one of the most dangerous. There are a lot of State murders and other violent crimes."

Looking out the truck window DJ thought they were driving through a junkyard. He never saw so many abandoned vehicles. Men were walking the streets openly carrying machetes. "It keeps getting worse." He thought.

They found the convenience store. Once again Chuks needed to do all the talking. DJ was on edge and the louder they spoke in their language, the more nervous he got.

It wasn't until they were safely back in the truck with the letters in hand that DJ's breathing returned to normal.

They decided it would be safer to travel back on the main roads. Once a safe distance from Kaduna they stopped at a small motel for the night.

~

He wasn't completely convinced when Chuks suggested he return to New York using the return ticket he already had. From there he should immediately board a flight to Ukraine. "This way there will be less wonder as to why you want to visit two different countries with corrupt governments" Chuks insisted.

There was still the issue of the $59,000 in cash he was carrying.

We need to visit a friend of mine in the morning who will send the cash ahead to New York for you, to a friendly business there. Once you are back home you can pick it up there. It will be safe.

His return flight to New York was booked by Levi for the following morning at 10:30 a.m. Chuks dropped him off at his original hotel in Lagos and instructed him to get food and spend the night in his room resting. "I'll pick you up at dawn, we'll take care of business and then get you to the airport on time."

Once his only friend in the country drove away, DJ felt so alone.

He enjoyed a spicy chicken and vegetables dinner in the hotel restaurant and ordered an assortment of fruit to bring to his room, for later.

Before going up to his room he went out front to catch the sunset. He had his fruit platter in one hand and his backpack hanging loosely on his other arm.

Two preteen boys came running and bumped aggressively into him sending his fruit sailing through the air as a third boy tried to rip the backpack off his arm. When DJ grabbed him by his hair the other two tried to wrestle the bag from his arm. *His id, his passport, the letters of credit and cash* were in the backpack. He panicked. Losing the money was one thing but losing the letters of credit, the reason he was there, and without his id he couldn't get home. He could not let these junior thugs ruin his plans! While he had the second boy by the hair the third was biting at his wrist and it hurt like hell. DJ punched him and the boy fell backwards, hitting his head on the sidewalk.

DJ put his size 13 Air Jordan on the kid's chest. The boy started to thrash around trying desperately to get away. DJ applied more pressure. The other two boys suddenly took off running as a soldier or police officer, DJ wasn't exactly sure, approached.

Without saying anything the officer grabbed the boy up from under D. J's foot nearly knocking him over. Quickly regaining his balance, DJ instinctively turned and walked quickly back into the hotel without looking back. All he could think of was Chuks telling him how corrupt the officers are in this country, and that they'll rob you and get away with it.

He jumped onto the elevator and pushed the fourth-floor button in case the officer was watching to see what floor he was on. He got off and found a stairway and hustled up to the fifth floor. He leaned against the door listening for any footsteps and only heard his own heart pounding. Opening the door slowly he slipped quietly into the hall and walked to the opposite side of the building where there was another staircase. He looked out the window and was able to see three officers standing under a streetlamp by the front entrance. His heart sank. The three of them appeared to be laughing. He took a deep breath and entered the stairway. He walked slowly up to the sixth floor, entered the hall, and made his way to the other end of the hall to his room.

There was no way he could see what was happening out front from his room.

While turning the faucet on for the shower he noticed his wrist was bleeding where one of the little bastards bit him. He also had scratches on his arms and shoulder. Leaning against the tile wall in the shower, he tried to catch his breath. The warm water felt so good. He started to relax but still didn't feel completely safe.

Packing was easy. There was only a small rolling carry-on bag and his backpack. The other backpack, the one holding the $50,000 would be prepared in the morning.

Deciding to wear his suit on the plane he ran an iron over the pants and hung them on the closet door. Counting out all his cash, he put $5000 in one pile. He would travel with this. Finding an envelope in the top drawer of the dresser, he placed $10,000 in the envelope and sealed it shut. He placed enough Nigerian currency to get something to eat and drink at the airport in the front compartment of his backpack. He hid the rest of the American money he would travel with under the cardboard bottom of his backpack.

He turned the television on, placed a wakeup call for 5:30 am and crawled under the covers on the kingside bed closest to the window. “Damn; I really wanted that fruit” he whispered to himself.

The ringing of the phone pierced his ears as he struggled to come out of the soundest, deepest sleep he ever had. Mumbling he told the clerk thank you and dropped the receiver on the floor.

Double checking his image in the mirror, he grinned. He pulled the backpack over his shoulders tightening the straps so it would be more difficult for someone to take from him.

As he stepped onto the elevator he was scared. He imagined the lobby filled with the military and the police. Relieved that there was nobody there other than a clerk behind the desk, he hurried through the front revolving door and rushed to the waiting taxi.

He opened the back door of the cab and said, “I’ve never been so happy to see someone in my life, my man!”

Chuks sped off and it seemed they were driving for quite some time when the largest brightest orange ball was all DJ could see. “What the hell is that!" He yelled. "Haven't you ever seen a sunrise before," Chuks said, laughing. "They don't make them like that in New Jersey!"

They travelled a bit longer. Rolling by Modern buildings, then much older buildings and now they were in an area of the country that was more like what DJ imagined. There were buildings with thatch roofs and structures were now rare.

When he pulled into a parking spot and told DJ to pull the back seat down and place his suitcase and the money he was going to be travelling with into the trunk. This made DJ extremely nervous. He eyed Chuks carefully looking for any sign that he might be planning something nefarious.

The two men walked up onto and then over a rickety wooden bridge. Once they got to the top the view was astonishing. The sun was resting on the entire ocean and the reflection on the water looked like thousands of tiny diamonds dancing in perfect rhythm with the softly rolling waves.

It took DJ's breath away. Taking his burner phone out of his jacket pocket he took a few photos hoping for the best because he was blinded by the brilliance making it impossible to see if he captured the photo.

"This is my gift for you Mr. DJ" Chuks said. He handed DJ a small plastic jar and instructed him to put some sand and a few shells in the container.

"You know something Chucks, I live in a beach town, and I don't even appreciate how blessed I am. I can't remember the last time I walked on the beach. It's fascinating that this is the same Atlantic Ocean that I see back home. Chucks explained to DJ that here in his country they were planning a manmade island and its name would be Atlantic City. Both men laughed realizing how small the world has become.

They walked along the water and in the distance DJ spotted five grass huts on the beach. As they got closer he smelled bacon and realized he was starving. They served it on skewers, sprinkled with sugar, and cooked on a grill. They each ordered three, an orange smoothie and an order of mixed fruit and sat on a nearby bench to eat.

"That's the best breakfast I've ever had." DJ said patting Chucks on the back.

A woman dressed in traditional clothing approached them and introduced herself as Gemma. She explained to DJ how she would transfer his cash to a business in New York for him. In exchange for her trouble, she would keep $10,000. At first DJ thought the amount was outrageously ridiculous but Chucks explained she took the time throughout the night to find companies here in country as well as businesses in America that would cooperate. This woman was taking a risk as a favor to Chuks.

Reluctantly DJ handed this stranger $44,000 in cash. All he could do was hope for the best at this point.

"I can't thank you enough my friend and I promise I will never forget you." DJ said. I'm going to leave you an envelope of cash." "I 'm so honored my friend." Chuks shook DJ's hand and said, "You are most generous my friend and I am forever grateful. May your journey be safe."

Holding tightly to the jar of sand until they pulled into the airport DJ couldn't believe how much had happened in less than forty- eight hours. He put the container of sand into his backpack. The two men hugged on the sidewalk and DJ whispered that he placed the cash along with his fare into the trunk.

He wasn't as lucky going through customs this time. DJs person and his bags were hand searched by an armed guard and they counted every dollar. Each of the three guards took a hundred dollars.

Grateful they only glanced at the pages of instructions he'd accumulated and that they didn't take all his cash, he put his belongings back into the bags and walked as quickly as he could to his gate.

He chose a seat as close to the jetway as he could find. It felt like every cop, guard or military person in the area was glaring at him. His mind kept trying to tell him they would pounce any moment. Trying not to make eye contact with anyone he focused on the large window and was able to see several planes lining up for takeoff.

He could not wait to feel his newly discovered feeling of freedom in the air.

Deciding a window seat was still the best idea, he put his roll on in the overhead compartment and his backpack under his feet. Men took both seats beside him. "This won't be fun," he mumbled.

Having slept through most of the thirteen- hour flight, DJ woke up starving. There was little chit chat with the two men seated beside him. They both seemed annoyed when he had to get up to use the rest room. His seat mates seemed even more annoyed when he returned. "I'm getting an aisle seat on the next flight!" He mumbled to himself.

He couldn't help wondering how his lady friends from the first flight were making out.

"Jimmy must be so worried," he said to himself, "I'm gonna call him soon."

After a rocky first meeting with Jimmy and an even worse second meeting DJ was surprised at how poorly he had prejudged him. Now he hoped his friend would understand why he had to take off and do this, why he couldn't say anything. It was the principle!

Customs was a breeze in New York, and he was so hungry, he decided on a steak dinner even though it was only 11:00 am in New York. While waiting for his meal to be served he decided to use his burner phone to find out what airline had a flight to Ukraine and when.

Ukraine International Airline had a nonstop flight leaving at 3:30 pm. He was lucky enough to get a ticket and an aisle seat.

As he sat at the gate waiting to board, he formulated a plan, sort of a plan.

"Why didn't I think to bring Chuks along?" He mumbled.

Chapter 13:
Ukraine

Trying to keep track of all the time changes was frustrating. The flight attendant announced it was 7:30 am in Kyiv. The good news was by the time he cleared customs the businesses should be open.

He scanned the lines and chose the one with the friendliest looking agents. There were no signs about cash, so he hoped he was okay.

Three hours later he was on the sidewalk in front of the airport waiting for a cab, hoping to get lucky with another friendly driver. It was ridiculously cold. Finally, a cab pulled up and he opened the back door and climbed in, hoping for the best.

When he asked the taxi driver if he was available for extra work, the driver emphatically answered no.

The young man explained there are two types of *taksis* in Ukraine. Official drivers that work for a large service, like him. Then there are private or independent drivers who drive around looking for fares at bus stops and airports. "Look for car with no sign, no lights on top." The driver explained in his best English. "These are getting harder to find locally because the government doesn't care for them. I don't care for them!"

Going out on a limb DJ asked if the non-company drivers sometimes aid travelers with less than above board business transactions.

The driver abruptly pulled off the highway and ordered DJ out of his car. "GET OUT" He shouted. Stunned DJ looked out the window at hundreds of cars whizzing by. He knew he had no choice. He opened the door, pulled his backpack over his shoulders. “My fare.” The driver demanded. Throwing a twenty- dollar bill on the back-seat DJ pulled his suitcase out and slammed the car door shut.

He had to carry his rolling bag because the highway shoulder was gravel. Looking straight ahead he tried to estimate how far he would need to walk to reach the next exit. Fear filled him, he couldn’t tell if he was in the city limits, or not.

A few cars slowed down to look him over.

The dress shoes he was wearing started to hurt and he was tired, hungry, and thirsty. At least the sun was brighter, and it was getting warmer.

He’d been walking for half an hour when a car pulled off the highway in front of him, nearly running him down.

As if in slow motion, the driver side door opened and an exceptionally tall and thin woman with shoulder length blonde hair got out and was walking towards him.

“Are you a taxi driver,” He asked, “A non- company driver?”

Her eyes were the prettiest, lightest shade of blue, he couldn’t help staring. “Tak,” She answered cracking the slightest smile. He must have looked confused because she then said, “Aye, yes.”

Relieved DJ asked if she was available to drive him. Smirking she said, “I stopped didn’t I.”

“Address?” DJ handed her the page with the name and address of the business he needed to get to. She gave him a sarcastic look and mumbled something he couldn’t make out. “Let’s go then.”

DJ hadn’t ridden in many cabs until now that is, it’s not an Atlantic City thing. He swore the car took two or three corners on two tires. This driver was batshit crazy!

She pulled up in front of the business and slammed the brakes. “Jesus,” DJ said, “Will you wait here?” “Yes, she answered while chugging vodka from one of those small bottles the airlines and hotels serve.

He wondered if he should tell her to go but decided he may need her help.

Before getting out of the car he looked over the business. On the left it looked like a small version of a 7-Eleven. Connected to the store was a concrete building that looked like a run down, office building.

After scanning the store employees, of course he went up to the only woman and again of course she was also the only one who was smiling. She looked at his papers and told him to wait.

DJ stood as close to the front door as possible in case he had to get out quickly.

At least twenty minutes passed. Two men finally appeared, one of them looking like Ivan Drago, the Russian boxer in the Rocky movies. They led him through a door and down a concrete hallway to an elevator. When they pressed the basement button, DJ started to sweat. He felt dizzy and nauseous.

“Why didn’t you make an appointment?” The shorter man shouted. “I apologize. I didn’t know I was supposed to.” “Next time call first.” The taller one said. “Okay.” DJ answered knowing full well he would not be coming back here, ever.”

The elevator door opened, and all DJ saw was concrete. “I’m gonna die.” He thought to himself. The men led him into an office where he signed several papers and was given another manilla envelope. The tall man then slammed three shot glasses on the desk and filled them with vodka. Not DJ’s favorite, but he knew he couldn’t disrespect them, so he slammed the shot, held his breath, and smiled.

"We'll transfer money to San Francisco and prepare $50,000 in cash for you here." The shorter guy said.

Another $50,000 in cash! DJ's head started to spin again. DJ couldn't help wondering what these guys already skimmed off the top.

"It should be available for you in California in two days. Until then, while you're here pay attention and be careful. Your people are not treated well in parts of this city. Absolutely under any circumstances do not go outside the city limits. It's extremely dangerous." The taller man instructed.

DJ assured them he was going straight to his hotel and staying put.

Yana, the driver waited for him. Although he was relieved DJ was also a bit terrified of what her meter would read. "Did you get what you went for?" She asked. "I made a deposit of some business checks. I must return to the airport in the morning, will you be available?" "Of course. Do you mind if I make a quick stop on the way back to your hotel?" He wanted to scream YES I MIND because I've been WARNED to stay in the hotel.

Instead, he said OKAY and off they went outside the city limits.

He had no choice but to ask for her help. "Yana how much cash can one fly out of Ukraine with?" "I think $10,000 US dollars unless you have permission from the bank." His heart sank and he struggled with the decision to ask the next question. Did he have a choice?

The woman didn't bat an eyelash. She knew exactly where to take him to have his cash wired to the United States.

She pulled into another convenience store and told him to wait.

He imagined he had to wait because it wasn't safe. It seemed like an hour that she was gone but was more like fifteen minutes. She returned and threw a bag to him in the back seat. She also handed him a cup of tea.

Let's go in. My friend will speak with you.

A woman instructed DJ to follow her and told Yana to wait outside. The two of them entered the smallest office DJ had ever seen. There wasn't a chair for him. The woman asked him how much cash he wanted to transfer and when he said $45,000 he knew by the expression on her face it was a much greater amount than what she normally dealt with. It took her a minute to gather her thoughts, but she agreed.

Twenty minutes later DJ left the small office with directions on retrieving the money once he was home. A part of the cash would be wired to San Francisco and the remaining cash would be sent to New York. The convenience store owner charged $10,000. DJ reminded himself of the risk these people took. Still, it was a lot of money.

He also planned to pay Yana for her help.

Once she sat in the driver's seat and started the cab she turned to him and held up a little plastic baggie of white powder. "You like?" she asked. He never wanted to say yes so bad in his life, but his gut shouted NO. "No thank you, I better not." He tried to sound firm.

She seemed disappointed. "Maybe back at your hotel," She asked. He said, "You're welcome to come back to my room," he said immediately regretting opening his mouth. "Okay," she said, "Let's go."

He peeked in the bag she threw to him when she first left the store. There were ten candy bars. *Candy Nut* bars. What a crazy name he thought. He opened one and it was good.

He was sure before the night was over he could be robbed of all his cash, but his common sense lost out to temptation before him. At that moment there was only this tall, blonde woman who was as terrifying as she was beautiful.

She snorted coke and he ordered room service, drank, and otherwise enjoyed her all night long. Every now and then he had a moment of clarity and looked over to make sure the safe was still securely closed and locked.

Yana drifted into what he was sure was a deep sleep, so he closed his eyes too.

Loud pounding on the door startled them both.

She put DJ's dress shirt on and looked through the doors peep hole. She mumbled something in Ukrainian. "What? Who is it?" DJ was wide awake now and filled with fear.

"It's the man who I was supposed to go back and pay for the coke." She sounded scared and that terrified DJ even more. "How much and will he take American money?" DJ asked.

He jumped off the bed, opened the safe and took out a thousand dollars and quickly locked it back up. He put a few hundred dollars on the dresser, in case the man insisted on more.

He pulled on his pants and sat in a chair by the window.

Yana opened the door. The man grabbed her by the throat and slammed her against the wall screaming at her in their language. DJ jumped up and shouted, "Is that necessary?" The man pushed DJ back into the chair grabbed the money from Yana's hand and took the money from the dresser too. Just like that he was gone.

After checking to make sure she wasn't hurt badly, DJ told Yana to order breakfast while he took a shower. While in the shower he gave himself a good talking too. "That is the last time I will ever do anything this crazy." He said to himself over, and over again until he at least half believed it.

Starving he reached for another one of the Candy Nut bars as he dressed. They were growing on him.

Yana showered and dressed. The two sat on the edge of the bed to eat breakfast. "Who was that guy? Why do you let him push you around like that and girl you should have told me you needed the money before we left the store, I would have given it to you to avoid this?"

She shook her head and didn't answer him.

"We have to go. I need to get to the airport."

After putting an envelope that held $1000 in her hand, he wished her the best and got out of the cab.

He hoped everything would go smoothly through customs. In all honesty he was afraid.

The young woman behind the airline ticket counter, the one with the smile instructed him to have a seat. As he waited he tried to remember what the heck happened the night before. He made a mental note not to drink vodka ever again for as long as he lived. These people had no aversion to drinking it with breakfast.

A short man with a military type of crew cut appeared and handed DJ his ticket and boarding pass.

Luck was on his side. Going through customs was a breeze.

Once at the gate he found a seat as close to the jetway as possible and kept his eyes on the window, watching planes coming and going.

He took his "real" phone out and called Jimmy.

After he screamed at him for making him think MS13 took him out DJ gave him the short version of the entire story.

"You can't keep that cash DJ, you're gonna get burned if you do, I promise!" "You just ripped off the wrong people. The kind of people that will have you swimming with the fishes."

This was not what DJ wanted to hear. His cop friend was bringing him down, and fast. "Jimmy I got the cash, some of it anyway and I know where to pick up the rest. No one will ever know," He pleaded his case, "I think I can pull it off."

Jimmy took a deep breath. You need to understand who these people are. It wouldn't matter if you stole twenty dollars or twenty million from them, they won't stop until they find you and kill you. Hopefully, it's only you they kill but they will wipe out your entire family.

"DJ didn't want to admit it but knew Jimmy was right and he didn't like it one bit!

"Let me talk to some people and see if I can get you out of this looking like a hero." He got DJ to tell him exactly where he was going in California and then made DJ promise to call him as soon as he got to San Francisco, before he did anything else.

~

The flight wasn't full. He had an aisle seat and no seat mates.

As nervous as he was about claiming his cash or not claiming his cash in San Francisco he was also looking forward to the weather. It had to be warmer than it was in Ukraine.

"However, this turns out damn straight I'm keepin my five- grand plus interest."

He pulled a Candy Nut bar out of his pocket, ate it, and fell asleep.

~

Chapter 14:
The Numbers Don't Add Up

In an office on the second floor of a middle eastern store front an Arab man sits at a desk. Three computer screens are open, but his eyes are on the window beside his desk and the magnificent view of the Nile River. He has spreadsheets lined up on a table in the center of the room. Realizing he's coming up negative on five accounts that are his responsibility to oversee, he starts to panic. Negative is not ever a word you ever want to mention to his bosses. He checked and then rechecked that the proper people signed the coded directories and the authorization documents so that the organizations cash to be withdrawn from each account.

They all lined up, except one. The account showing an unauthorized withdrawal of funds for the sum of $800,000 US dollars was from a bank account in Nigeria that was set up in a hacked and random American's name.

Once sure that there was a breach he sent an email to a compound near the border of Syria. The communications commander read the message, took out a piece of paper and wrote a note. He gave it to a young boy who was waiting patiently in the lobby, hoping for a message to deliver. In Arabic he gave the boy detailed instructions and the location of the commander who would be waiting for the message.

The kid was driven to a location closer to the border and he was given a knapsack that held water bottles, a container of chicken and vegetables, some fruit, and a few pitas.

From there he traveled alone on foot to avoid check points.

It took the child 3 days of walking in an active war zone to reach the commander. The random gunfire and shelling didn't affect the child. In his ten short years it was all he knew.

As the commander read the note he became physically agitated. He surmises that a rival group must have stolen the money and were now planning to use it to purchase weapons. His group recently entered, into a deal with the Russians, but they didn't finalize the deal, yet.

After ranting for what seemed like hours, he gave the note to another soldier in the compound and ordered him in Arabic to have Samid Nasir lead an investigation into this unauthorized expenditure, the betrayal.

He then wrote and signed a note and handed it to the boy who was shaking. The kid put the note in his underpants and took off running, as fast as he could, weaving his way in and out of bombed buildings.

With his back up against the corner of a concrete building, he slowly inched his head around the corner. It was clear. He waited. Two minutes later he looked again. Taking a deep breath, he took off running and ran smack into an American soldier. After an awkward moment of silence, the kid raises his hands in the air and yells, "I refugee, I refugee."

Aggravated because his mission would take longer the soldier grabbed the kid's hand and ran with him while using his radio to call for aid. A hummer finally pulled up and the soldier tossed the kid onto the backseat and shut the door. The kid watched as the soldier took off running back in the direction they came from as the hummer drove off.

Relaxed because they didn't search him again and knowing the urgent note was safe in his underpants, he sat back against the seat and grinned. He knew they'd give him a hot meal and a bag of American candy before they delivered him to a refugee camp found in a safer area but still along the Syrian border.

Standing in line for yet another meal the kid nodded, as he was taught to do towards an Arab serving the food at the camp.

When that server finished, he went to a section of the camp where Arab soldiers ate together. He gave a nod to one of the soldiers standing guard and that soldier placed his hat visibly on a windowsill.

The following morning, a woman dressed in full burka identified the boy as her nephew, Mahdi. When the kid acknowledged her, she was handed documents to sign. The two of them were released from the camp and they walked together into a small town seven miles from the camp to her home.

She made Mahdi a cup of tea and made a phone call. An hour later the boy was picked up by two men.

Two men along with the boy traveled by pick-up truck well into the night, leaving the main road to avoid approaching check points. Mahdi slept.

By midday they reached the capitol and pulled up in front of a travel agency.

The boy, still groggy got out and went into the agency. A clerk directed him to a large back room. He walked up to the managers desk and seeing the man was on the phone he proudly dropped the note in a message basket. Without taking his eyes off his computer screen or his phone off his ear the man said in Arabic, "God's little worrier come back here." The boy grinned from ear to ear and ran back to the desk. Lifting the boy onto his lap the manager opened his desk drawer and pulled out a large chocolate bar. "You've been guided along the right path. I will pray for your safety." He put the boy down. They shook hands and the boy skipped back to the car. Once safely in the back seat he opened the candy bar and ate the entire thing.

Before the boy interrupted him the travel agency manager was busy attaching various naked pictures to emails.

He pulled the note out of the basket, typed an email, and attached a naked photo. In the subject bar he typed "Can you find what's missing here?"

At yet another office in another middle eastern country a man opened the email, read the message, and opened the photo in a program that allowed editing. Enlarging the photo, he was able to see pixel distortion and changes in color. He clicked down 850 fragments and then over 452. Once at 452 he was able to clearly see a message. He copied it and then enlarged the copy. The letter had the country, the bank, and the stolen identification that they used to open the account. It also had information on the guy the group used to open the account with the stolen identification.

He made a phone call and twenty minutes later six men picked up the information and then headed to the airport to catch a flight to Nigeria.

A driver was waiting for them in Lagos and took them straight to the bank.

The bank manager received a text message saying that there would be a meeting. Not knowing the reason for the meeting, he nervously awaited their arrival.

Cooperating with their demands he gave them the names and addresses of the companies that agreed to guarantee and to wire the money. He assured the intimidating group of six that he was sure the man was a group mule. Seeing they weren't satisfied he mentioned the man originally had a list of Jewish companies he wanted to use to transfer the cash.

The lead investigator asked the manager for copies of the man's identification. "Did this man speak our language?" "No." The banker answered. "Why didn't you realize something wasn't right when he didn't speak the language and of all things he wanted to do business with Jews?" The investigator shouted. The banker had no answers. "Please tell me you recorded the transportation he used." "Yes, my guard took photos. He left in a taxi." The banker answered slightly relieved that he finally had a good answer. The banker instructed his assistant to pull the photos of the cab from the file.

"Get those transfers stopped immediately!" The investigator shouted before turning and walking out of the bank.

The manager was relieved, but it was fleeting. He knew it was too late to stop the transfers and that might have sealed his fate. He sat at his desk and with his head in his hands and tried to come up with a solution.

A few hours later the squad pulled up to Chuks house. He was in his yard changing the oil on his cab. The six men interrogated the taxi driver. Chuks caught on quick that they wanted his new friend DJ He firmly told them all he did was take him to the bank. "I waited outside. When he came out I took him to a hotel."

One of the investigators walked up behind Chuks and put a gun to his neck. Two of the others walked close to a tree where three of Chucks smaller children were playing and yelled, Get in the house."

At that moment he knew these men were not only there to intimidate him. Another man slammed the hood of the taxi down on Chuks hand. It took every ounce of inner strength he had, not to scream. He didn't want to frighten his kids.

He'd held out for as long as he could. The pain in his hand and the intense fear he felt for his family's safety he gave them every detail he remembered about his fare that day.

He told them he was an American and lived in a place called Atlantic City, in New Jersey.

The squad was confused. Convinced it was a rival group that robbed them and not some American they knew Chuk's was lying. They forced him into the house and brutally stabbed each of his family members to death one by one including the children. When Chuck's continued to insist it was an American they cut out his tongue, and then beheaded him.

When finished, the squad washed up and went to a restaurant to have supper.

While on his way home that night terrorist ran the bank managers vehicle off road, and they beheaded him. The squad then went to his house and blew it up with his family inside.

The squad still had no clear idea of who the rival group was and that wasn't going to go over well with their commanders.

To relieve tension, they joked about the possibility of the thief being an American. "The taxi driver was clever to imagine that story. They laughed.

~

The messenger boy received a little money and then they dropped him off to the woman in the burka. She delivered the boy to his parents. They were proud of their little entrepreneur.

Chapter 15:
San Francisco

DJ slept the entire flight. One of the attendants gently patted his shoulder. "We're approaching LAX sir. Would you like a coffee?" DJ walked to the back of the plane to use the restroom, splash some water on his face and comb his hair.

Once back in his seat the attendant returned with almond cookies and a coffee.

He didn't have much time to catch his connecting flight to San Francisco, he was grateful the gate wasn't too far.

Feeling like he was still in the middle of a toss-up between a nightmare and a dream come true, he checked in for the next flight and found a seat. Looking out the window he couldn't believe what he was seeing. He asked a young woman seated to the left of him, "Is that the plane we're taking?" The girl got a kick out of the question and giggled. "Don't worry I take this trip often." "It's so little." The girl giggled again. "It is small but it's fast. You'll be fine."

Someone left a San Francisco Today magazine on the seat to the right of him. Hoping to read something that would take his mind off the small plane he thumbed through the pages and discovered the end of April is the best time to visit San Fran.

With highs of 63 degrees and average lows around 49 degrees, the weather is perfect. There's a boat parade on the bay, a Cherry Blossom festival, a film festival, and flower shows. Artists gather at a shipyard and display their work.

After the arctic weather in Ukraine, San Francisco sounded fabulous.

First he had to walk down the jetway and get on that plane. He kept telling himself it would only be an hour and a half flight. After flying around the world this would be a breeze.

That turned out to be just another lie he told himself. Now he was well versed on turbulence and was more scared than he'd been to walk into that first bank in Africa to steal his money back.

The young girl continued to laugh at him throughout the flight. "I might kiss the ground when we land." He told her.

San Francisco was chillier than that damned magazine said it would be. It was so windy. DJ decided to check into a hotel, shower and get something to eat before going to the places on his list to collect his cash.

While waiting for room service to arrive with his breakfast DJ decided to call Ezee. "DJ where the hell have you been?" "My uncle passed I had to go to his funeral in California. I have a big favor to ask. Can you pick me up at Newark Airport tomorrow night? My flight gets in at 8:00. I'll explain when I see you, I promise."

Ezee hated the two- hour trip up the Garden State Parkway, especially in his old work truck. It was a gas hog and the tools rattled making it noisy as hell, but he said yes.

"DJ are you sure you're okay?" "Better than okay. Wait till you hear. I gotta go my breakfast is finally here."

Deciding that at the bank via ride share would be less conspicuous than a cab, DJ used his burner phone and a Visa gift card to order a Lyft.

While waiting for his ride he wondered into the hotel gift shop and bought a pair of sunglasses.

The bank and businesses were located on the same block. He had the Lyft driver drop him off at a Starbucks located across the street from the bank.

He walked a block and a half to a custom furniture store and asked to see the owner. A cheerful middle-aged woman with bright red hair piled on top of her head appeared from behind a curtain made from beads. "Follow me." DJ couldn't help but think of the Bible story, *Coat of Many Colors,* as he followed her down a long narrow hallway. She explained to him that after cutting hundreds of triangles out of scrap material she had laying around, she stitched them together and the coat was the result.

"Who does that?" DJ thought to himself. Once seated in her office he took the paperwork from his backpack and handed it to her.

Ten minutes later he was back out on the sidewalk with $18,000 tucked away in his backpack. Trying not to smile, because he knew he'd look like a Cheshire cat, he put his head down and followed the sidewalk up a hill and around a corner.

If he quit now and headed to the airport, he'd be a winner. Giving that idea up without a second thought he kept walking. He stopped in front of the clock store to admire the watches in the window.

Once inside he cringed a bit when he saw the middle eastern man behind the counter dressed in a white thobe and kufi. He approached the man and asked for the owner. When the man told DJ he was the owner, DJ handed him the paperwork.

"Give me a few minutes." The man said and he disappeared through a door.

A watch in one of the display cases caught DJ's eye. It was simple, plain but there was something special about it. When the man reappeared DJ asked the man if he could see the watch. "Of course."

He handed DJ an envelope with $18,000 inside and then slid the watch out of the case.

"It's a Jaegar-LaCoulre. This one, Master Moon 39 is a masterpiece. It maps the phases of the moon. As you can see it's sleek, ultra- thin and is elegant." "How much." DJ asked expecting to hear $1200. "This watchmaker based in Switzerland has been creating luxury watches since 1833. It retails for between $13,000 and $19,000."

"Woah." Was all DJ could come up with. "For you a special deal, today only $8000. Look at this elegant detail, silver hour markers and blue second counters. It is unique."

Not caring if it was real or fake DJ put the watch on his wrist and held his arm out, admiring the watch. "Sold." He took $8000 out of the envelope and handed it back to the man he now knew as Sam.

They shook hands and DJ hit the sidewalk again, this time headed back toward the Starbucks. He was hungry. After ordering an iced coffee and a sandwich he found an empty table, sat down, and considered what he should do with his backpack. He placed it on the seat beside him and slid the stool under the table.

Seated next to him were two men dressed in navy blue suits with red ties. Both had earpieces. He smiled to himself thinking they looked like FBI agents. Both men were speaking but not to each other and both were looking at the bank across the street. The very bank DJ was going to, after lunch.

About three bites in he was shocked as he watched five SUV's pull up in front of the bank and the passengers got out with guns pointed towards the bank entrance.

"Is that bank getting robbed?" He said loud. One of the blue suits answered. "No, it's getting busted."

DJ couldn't think of anything other than he was never so grateful for his stomach. He could only imagine what could have happened if he were inside that bank and not sitting in Starbucks having lunch.

Minutes later an ambulance and a half dozen police cruisers rolled up to the bank. DJ lost count at thirteen people led out in handcuffs. "What'd they do?" He asked loud again. This time there was no answer. The two men got up and left. Through the window he watched as they walked down the sidewalk, away from the bank.

Holding his arm out he admired his watch again. Guilt was setting in. That money would've bought a lot of groceries, clothes, and toys for his kids. Still, he never bought anything so nice for himself, ever.

Back to reality he watched the buzz happening outside and realized there was no way he was going to that bank to collect money. "At least all the other pick-ups are in New Jersey.

He bought a pack of chocolate covered nuts and a pack of cookies and walked outside. Not sure if he should glare at the commotion across the street or ignore it he did a little of both as he walked down the sidewalk towards the bay. The view reminded him of home. He found a bench and shared his cookies with a bunch of pushy pigeons.

Once the cookies were gone he ordered a Lyft to take him back to the airport.

Happy to be going home but coming to the realization that it was still dangerous for him in Atlantic City. He was quite sure MS13 was too stupid to figure out it was him that stole their money. If he was being honest it was multiple victim's money he stole back from them. He was also sure they still had a hit out on him because his wife owed them money or because she was sleeping with one of them.

He was going to have to face Jimmy. "Jimmy! Oh my God I forgot to have Ezee ask him to meet me at the warehouse, to let me in."

Packing didn't take long. Double checking to make sure he grabbed his phone charger; he placed the room key on the dresser and closed the door to the last hotel room he wanted to see for a long time.

On his way to the Delta gate, he stopped by a newsstand and bought a few newspapers and a bottle of water for the flight.

"What?" He says to himself as he read the headline. ***80 Arrested in Identity Theft Sting***.

Chapter 16:
The FBI

Relieved that he would be flying to Newark on a real plane, a big one, he found a seat and finished reading the article.

San Francisco-*80 Defendant's arrested in International Takedown of Massive Conspiracy to steal Millions!*

Arrests were made in Los Angeles, San Francisco, and various locations in Nigeria.

DJ couldn't believe what he was reading. There was no mention of MS13, so he doubted this had anything to do with any of the people, banks, or businesses he visited. He was sure the bank he almost went to was involved.

The eighty defendants were involved in various romance and financial internet schemes most targeting the elderly, defrauding them of millions of dollars.

The syndicate targeted in the United States and across the globe including individuals. Law firms, and various businesses.

Once a victim made a deposit the defendant's coordinated with an international network to launder the funds. The money was wired to other banks in the network using the identifications of identity theft victims. Cash was also withdrawn as cashier's checks.

With stolen cash the defendant's used money exchangers known as mules to apply for Nigerian bank wire transfers.

The FBI led this investigation.

"Billions of dollars are stolen each year, and we are urging people to be aware of these sophisticated scams and to protect themselves and their businesses from becoming victims. The FBI is committed to working with agencies worldwide to identify these criminals and to take down their illicit networks."

Several agencies took part in this investigation including the Postal Service, U.S. Customs and Border Protection, the IRS, Homeland Security, many District Attorney Offices, the National Crime Agency in the United Kingdom, the Public Prosecutor in Germany and the Economic and Financial Crimes Commission in Nigeria.

As he stood in line waiting to board he gave Ezee a call and asked him to pick up the warehouse key from Jimmy. "Thank you again Ezee. I know driving to Newark is a hassle. I owe you big time man!" DJ clicked his phone off and made his way down the jetway.

Too excited to nap DJ read both newspapers entirely and was still a bit stunned over the coincidences.

Even if Jimmy did understand why DJ didn't tell him where he was going, he was still going to be pissed-off. It was decided, he had to tell him.

Although he was thrilled to be home and in one piece it still felt strange. Walking through the Newark Airport felt surreal. Most noticeable was the fact that there were no military personal pointing weapons at anyone.

In the past hearing people say things like, "It feels so good to be back on American soil." Made him laugh. He thought they were being overly dramatic. In this moment though, he felt something real and quite profound. It felt like home, and he felt safe for the first time in weeks. "It's a thing." He thought as he took a few deep breaths and walked through the automatic glass sliding doors and looked for Ezee's truck. Spotting him in the outer lane, he hustled across the street.

"I've never been so happy to see you." DJ laughed. "It's a two- hour drive and I'm all ears," Ezee started, "Where the hell have you been?"

"I'll explain all of that," DJ started, "But first will you do me another huge favor?"

DJ asked Ezee to drive into New York so he could drop a letter off to a cousin that worked in a convenience store in Brooklyn. This was one of the stores that DJ's cash was sent to, the one with the largest amount of cash he'd be able to collect in the States.

The pick-up was too easy. DJ shook a bit through the entire transaction, but he walked out of the store with $22,000.00 in cash.

During the long ride back to Atlantic City, DJ spilled the whole story to Ezee, except for the part about picking up the cash in Brooklyn.

"What? You have balls, I gotta give you that. Who does that crazy shit?" Ezee laughed and laughed. "I had to Ezee. Those guys deserved to get stung. No two ways about it. They deserved it."

"Are you sure it was MS13. It seems like a sophisticated scam for them to have pulled off. In case you haven't noticed, they ain't that smart." "Who else would it be?" DJ. wondered aloud. "Speaking of MS13, they've been around and they ain't playing. Jimmy said that FBI friend of his wanted to talk to you about it. You should talk to him. There really isn't any other way. It's putting all of us in danger." Ezee lectured. "I hear you and I'm gonna talk to him. Did Jimmy give you the key?" "Yep, he gave me the key and he isn't happy." "I figured."

DJ went on to explain to Ezee how the process worked. All he had to do now was go to thirty different convenience stores in the Atlantic City area to pick up his cash.

"I don't know DJ it all seems to have gone too smoothly. Watch your back."

"Silly question, Ezee. Has Deasia been by the house? Have you seen her?" "Sorry DJ, I haven't seen her. There has been someone sitting in front of your house 24/7 though. You need to stay away."

"I been thinking about that house," DJ started, "My cousin asked if he could rent the house for a few weeks. He got out of prison and needs a place to be with his girl and kids until he gets on his feet. Maybe if the gang realizes I'm no longer there, they'll go away."

Ezee thought it was a good idea, so DJ called his cousin and told him where the spare key was.

After dropping DJ off at the warehouse, Ezee texted Jimmy to let him know.

Using his "real" phone, DJ texted Levi. MISSION ACCOMPLISHED! I'll call you tomorrow.

DJ called his cousin to make sure he got into the house okay. Hearing the happiness in his cousin's voice, DJ was sad. Being away, having so much to do and being under so much stress, it had been easier not to think about how much he missed his family and his home.

He turned on the T.V. and watched the local news. When that ended he walked around the shop, examining the finished work. Coming across a set of cabinets that needed to be sanded some more he put on a mask and turned on the sander. When he finished, he cleaned up the mess and decided to try to get sleep.

~

Banging nearly caused DJ to fall off the cot. He stumbled to the door and opened it for Jimmy. Grateful for the coffee but not ready for what was coming next, DJ sat at the kitchen island. He took the lid off his coffee cup and added four packets of sugar and four creamers.

"I thought they took you out you stupid bastard. That was my first thought. Not cool DJ You could have called. Why didn't you at least call or text me?"

"Sit down DJ Tell me everything."

"Are you telling me you went to Africa, Ukraine, and California? That you defrauded the scammers? DJ they aren't going to take to being stung by you lying down. You're in more danger than ever. Seriously you aren't shittin me, you went to Africa by yourself!"

DJ pulled out his burner phone and showed Jimmy the photographs he took.

"So, tell me who knows you went?" "You, Ezee and my old boss Levi. He helped me out with contacts over there. I promised to cut him in. His contacts didn't work out, but I couldn't have done any of it without his help." That's it. I joked about it at work, but those guys don't know I actually did it." "Good," Jimmy said, "Keep it that way. Tell no one. And stay the hell in here!"

Jimmy had no idea what to make of DJ's story. It was either the craziest thing he ever heard or the gutsiest. As much as he was a major pain in his ass, he was relieved DJ was back and in one piece. Business was picking up, so he needed his help in the shop too.

How was he going to tell DJ he couldn't keep the money?

Two days later Jimmy's FBI friend Frank stopped by the shop.

Jimmy first met Frank at the police department. After he suffered injuries in an accident while on duty, Jimmy went to work with a task force. His job was to listen to wire taps.

He was good with technology and concocted a way for everyone in the wire room to be able to hear conversations.

It was his ex-partner Tommy who listened in on those conversations and used some of the information to implicate Jimmy in all sorts of wrongdoing.

He also accused Jimmy of pulling strings with the code enforcement office, to get a woman to lower the price on a house he wanted to buy as an investment. It never happened and Jimmy was able to prove to it to Frank.

When he removed the roof on the property, there were only thirty-five tresses. There should have been seventy. The house could've collapsed.

It was Frank who told Jimmy, they finally got Tommy and the judge sentenced him to ten-years in prison. The two have been friends ever since.

Frank loved reminding Jimmy that he was the agent that cleared him. "Remember me, I'm the agent that cleared you!" "You didn't clear me of anything," Jimmy answered, "Because I didn't do anything."

They spoke outside the warehouse. "Your buddy, DJ was in L.A. the other day. Didn't you tell me MS13 used the IRS fraud on him? Are you sure he wasn't in on the fraud and are you positive it was the gang bangers? Money scams haven't been their MO and if it is now we're on to something here."

Jimmy was surprised. He invited Frank into the warehouse.

"It couldn't have been DJ. I know he hasn't left this building in days. There's no way it was him."

The two men decided MS13 sold his identification, and it was used by a hired double, or it was the simple coincidence of two guys with the same name.

Brushing talk of DJ aside, the agent told Jimmy they had some decent leads on Deasia and the kids. They also knew the identity of Raffa, and he was a big want for Homeland and the FBI. Let's not say anything to him until I know some more.

DJ walked across the large room and reached into the refrigerator for a beer. "Grab two more." Jimmy asked.

"DJ this is a friend, Frank.." The two men shook hands. "You 5-0 too?" DJ asked in his typical sarcastic tone. "Sort of." Frank answered matching the sarcastic tone. "Nice to meet you man." DJ said as he walked back to his makeshift bedroom.

"So that was him?" "Yep." Jimmy answered.

The two finished their beers and Frank told Jimmy he'd be back in a day or two with more information.

Jimmy couldn't stop thinking about what Frank said about it not being MS13 that scammed DJ the gang was trying to kill him, that was a fact but some of the other pieces weren't exactly fitting together.

Chapter 17:
Time to Get Paid

"Levi, the best thing about this whole thing is all the locations left on my list are here in New Jersey, many are right here in A.C. And most of them are convenience stores or gas stations, many of them on the same block. I feel so much safer than I did going into those big companies overseas. One of them is the Seven- Eleven I've been getting my coffee from for years." DJ said. "That's all well and good," Levi said, "But don't let your guard down for one second. Be aware of everything around you."

Early the next morning DJ put on a Giant's baseball cap, a blue zip up hoodie and walked the four and a half blocks to that Seven- Eleven Store where he's always gotten his coffee.

"Where have you been my friend?" The clerk greeted him. He went on to ask about his divorce, his kids, and his job. "It's all working out," DJ answered, "I was granted custody of my kids. Hopefully, they'll be with me soon. How's your family?" DJ asked as he handed the clerk the credit certificate.

The clerk, a bit startled at first because this wasn't something DJ was normally involved with and suspecting his longtime customer may be setting him up for the police, he asked, "Where did you get this?"

DJ suddenly felt like he'd been stopped by the cops with weed on him and a suspended license. He knew to stay as calm, cool, and collected as possible and not to tell the truth.

"My boss asked me to take care of this for him, you know because I live in the neighborhood. He doesn't trust many people with his money."

"The Jewish guy you worked for before? You're working for him again?" The clerk asked. "Yea someone owes him on a bad loan. He hired me to do the pick-ups."

"Fucking Jews," The clerk said causing DJ to step back. "Always taking advantage of Muslims." "How do you know it's a Muslim paying him?" "Because of where the slip came from, this would only be a Muslim."

Trying to play off any suspicion DJ said, "None of it matters to me, I get paid to be his delivery boy, I need the money and I got to go before I'm late."

The clerk opened his safe and counted out $4000 and handed it to DJ "Have a good day my friend." "Thank you." DJ said. He left the store and walked halfway down the block before he cracked half a smile. That was a bit tougher than he thought it would be, but it was America.

Patting his pocket that held the cash, he whistled as he walked towards his next stop. This place was a mom & Pop dollar type store.

The boy behind the counter smiled and said, "Good morning." As DJ walked in. He waved.

Trying to be as inconspicuous as possible he grabbed an orange juice from refrigerator and a granola bar from the candy aisle and placed them on the counter. After paying the cashier, he handed him the credit slip. Without flinching he opened the register drawer and counted out $4000 and handed it to him.

Relieved, he opened the granola bar and started walking towards his next stop, another mom & Pop convenience store. He handed the young man behind the counter the credit slip. He told him to hold on as he sent a text.

DJ picked up a newspaper off the rack and pretended to read the front page, trying to calm his nerves. "Am I pressing my luck trying to get too much at once?" he wondered.

An elderly man appeared and asked to see the credit slip. "You the new man?" He asked. "Filling in." DJ answered sounding as confident as he could. He spoke to the cashier in their language, nodded to DJ and walked away. The young man handed him $4000.

He made his way back to the warehouse hoping Jimmy hadn't noticed he was gone. The coast was clear, barely.

Within minutes Jimmy arrived and asked DJ to put on a pot of coffee.

DJ showed Jimmy the work he did the night before. "Couldn't sleep huh?"

"Nah I slept on the flight from California. Jimmy I want you to know I planned all along to cut you in. I have no idea how it will all play out or how much I'll end up getting but I'd never leave you out." DJ said as he spread the $12,000 he collected that morning on the island.

"Put that away before one of the guys comes in and see's it." Jimmy yelled. "I can't believe you went out, you idiot!"

Jimmy's gut was telling him there was so much more to this and he was positive things could go very wrong if he wasn't careful. He double checked the weapons he placed strategically around the shop, and he added some rope and a couple of knives.

With the weather getting warmer his employees sometimes opened a side door that led to an alley. Jimmy told them to keep that door closed and locked to put on the air conditioning and fans if it got too hot.

Chapter 18:
Miami

Deasia and DJ often talked about, even dreamed of taking their kids to Disney World one day. Instead, her and the kids did a drive by of the happiest place on Earth. "Florida has to be one of the longest states." She thought. The ride from Jacksonville to Miami seemed endless, especially with three kids who were hot, tired, and starting to question incessantly where their dad was, especially six-year-old Jasmine. She was her father's little princess and she missed him.

When they finally arrived at Raffa's cousins house in Hialeah, Deasia tried to summon a positive attitude, but it wasn't easy. Maria, Raffa's cousin's wife wasn't welcoming to say the least. They weren't there for an hour when Raffa and his cousin Manny left to 'take care of business.'

Maria never offered Deasia or the kids so much as a glass of water, not even after she asked for walking directions to a convenience store.

Her and the kids walked three blocks and found a large Mom and Pop corner store. The Hispanic clerks were friendly and helped the kids pick out a snack and a drink.

Deasia asked how far they were from the beach. "It's about fourteen-miles from here." A young woman who appeared to be in her late teens explained.

As they walked the three blocks back to Maria and Manny's house Deasia was having serious second, even third thoughts about being here. She had no idea how to get herself and the kids out of this disaster she created.

She was sure Raffa wouldn't let her leave and there was no way she could take off because there was no way she could get her hands on the money she'd need to get home. There was no way she could even call anyone for help because he threw her phone out of the window in North Carolina. Raffa said the police could trace and find them through the cell phone. He promised to get her a new one but that hadn't happened, yet.

When Raffa returned he told her Manny's brother Michael was arrested for shooting a sheriff deputy in the face during a confrontation. Luckily, the cop didn't die.

Sheriffs were trying to serve a narcotic's warrant when the confrontation on another family member's house and car when the homeowner pulled a gun on a deputy. The homeowner was at once shot by four of the officers and killed. Michael shot one of the deputies.

Michael's been in trouble before. His arrests included burglary, drug possession, illegal fire-arm possession, drug possession and resisting arrest. He was let go from prison a few months before and the family hoped he'd lay low at least for a little while.

The deputy's shooting prompted Immigration and Customs Enforcement (ICE) to arrest twenty-six other gang members which was hurting MS13's operations. On top of operations affected the timing was horrible because tensions were high between MS13, the Bloods and Nortenos an affiliate of a Northern California gang trying to plant roots in South Florida. All were jockeying to become the leader in sex and human trafficking, narcotics smuggling, murder, and racketeering.

That morning one of MS13's South Florida leaders was arrested and already deported to El Salvador where he was wanted on ten-year-old rape charge.

Manny was worried they were coming for him next for his involvement in the abducting of two seventeen-year-old girls that escaped and would be able to find him.

The two men decided they would sell the brand- new car they bought with DJ's credit to a chop shop and use the money to buy a van. Deasia and Raffa would drive Manny, a pregnant Maria, and their three-year-old daughter to Texas where Maria had family.

Another long road trip with now four kids was the last thing in the world Deasia wanted to take. Raffa convinced her it would be fun.

She also realized giving up the car that was technically DJs was another piece of freedom being taken from her. At times she felt so overcome with guilt for taking the kids from DJ the kids missed him so much, she hadn't expected them to react that way.

Once Raffa took her into the bedroom and hooked her up with a much- needed fix, she was more agreeable.

The two men left the women again to arrange the car switch. Maria packed. Deasia felt the slightest twinge of sorrow for her. She knew what it was like to leave a nice home and everything she ever knew for a life on the run.

Raffa promised to take the kids to the beach. Now he had to explain to them they would be stopping at the beach when they were halfway to Texas. He also promised them they could ride horses in Texas.

"Are we going to be safe, will the kids be safe?" Deasia asked Raffa for reassurance. "We will be okay, I promise." He answered.

The plan was to get sleep and leave around 4:00 a.m. If everything went well, they'd be in Panama Beach by 1:00 p.m. This would give them the afternoon to let the kids run and play on the beach. They would spend the night and leave early in the morning again, and arrive in Houston by 3:00 p.m.

Deasia felt sick to her stomach when she saw the I-95 sign. Part of her wanted to head north and keep going with her kids as fast as she could, and another part never wanted to see New Jersey again as long as she lived. She closed her eyes and tried not to think at all.

They went through the McDonalds drive thru for breakfast once the kids were fully awake.

All along the highway construction was happening which caused several areas of congestion. It didn't slow them down too much, they arrived in Panama at 2:00 p.m.

The hotel they chose was beachfront and it had a pool. A half hour after arriving the kids were jumping waves and building sandcastles. They were all smiles.

After they splurged on an oceanfront steak dinner, the kids and the grownups swam in the pool until 8:00 p.m. Everyone was exhausted and the plan was to get up and be on the road by 4:00 a.m.

"Drive the speed limit, you know what they say about Alabama." Deasia warned. She gave the same warnings as they entered Mississippi and Louisiana. Shortly after crossing into Texas, they stopped for a long lunch, and they found a park to let the kids stretch their legs.

"How long will we be in Houston?" Deasia asked. Raffa looked at Manny before answering. "Not sure yet." He answered.

Manny's mood started to darken back in Louisiana and the closer they got to Houston the meaner he seemed to get. He shouted at Maria when she asked to stop at a rest area. It was upsetting to Deasia because Maria was seven-months pregnant. It wasn't good for her or the baby to be sitting down for so long. His yelling most certainly wasn't good for them either. When Deasia nicely asked Manny to please stop yelling at Maria he shouted at her also.

Raffa clearly didn't like his cousin treating his girl that way and firmly told him to chill. It worked for a while, but it was clear that everything that had happened was catching up to Manny and he was scared.

When Raffa told Deasia, they would be staying at a motel and not at Maria's aunts house, Deasia was relieved. When the kids saw the pool at the motel they were thrilled.

~

Frank, Jimmy's FBI agent buddy received a call from the Miami-Dade Sheriff's office. He was told they had eyes on the brother of a cop shooter. The Miami agent texted Frank a photo of a couple staying at the shooters house. He was wondering if Frank could find the couple.

"The guy is suspected MS13, and he's wanted for questioning in a couple of shootings here in New Jersey. Do they have kids with them?" "Yes, not sure of how many but a few." "The woman took off with the kids, her husband has full custody. The problem is he hasn't reported her missing, yet. I'm working on that. If possible hold them and give me a heads up."

The sheriff's department surrounded Manny's neighbor's home. They were trying to serve a search warrant for the house and a vehicle. The neighbor pulled a gun and tried to flee on foot. By the time, the Sheriff's realized their mistake, both couples were long gone.

They put a BOLO (be on the lookout) for Deasia's car. When they didn't receive a single call on a sighting of the car, they were confused.

Frank hoped for DJ's sake the worst hadn't happened. It was MS13 they were talking about.

~

The motel was only a few blocks from Maria's aunt's house, but it may as well have been in the middle of nowhere. Raffa and Manny were gone day and night which left Deasia alone with the kids, with no car and sometimes no food.

When he finally returned he was the big hero, bursting in the motel room with fast food or pizza and candy, lots of candy.

The next day would be more of the same.

More than once Deasia considered stealing money and the car keys. She'd seen enough the last few weeks to know she wouldn't get far, unless she came up with a good plan. As hard as it was she had to admit to herself that she was a heroin addict and wouldn't get far before getting sick. Besides that, Raffa was MS13 with connections all over the country. She wouldn't make it out of the county.

Sitting on a chaise, by the motel pool she decided the first thing she had to do was stop using. Cold turkey was out of the question. She would start with one less hit each day. Watching the kids splash in the pool and play with other kids, she couldn't help smiling.

When Raffa returned to the hotel that night she told him her plan to get clean. He laughed at her. It was a different side of him. For years she accused DJ of controlling her and here she was allowing this man to control her by keeping her in need of drugs. Disgusted with herself, she stormed out of the motel room and walked until she was crying.

Raffa never came after her and when she returned to the motel room he was sound asleep. She cried herself to sleep.

Normally she shot up eight times within twenty-four hours. By the end of that week, she was down to six-times. She was determined to show him and herself that she was serious.

The more sober and serious about sobriety she became, the meaner Raffa became.

They'd been at the motel for two weeks when Raffa came into the room at 2:00 a.m. and announced they had to leave, at once. He started throwing their stuff into a bag and shouting for the kids to wake up.

By 2:30 a.m. they were back on the highway. I-10 East was still under construction but at the late or early hour it wasn't too bad. At 4:30 the kids were up and whining and Raffa was exhausted and clearly anxious about something, but he wasn't talking.

At 6:00 a.m. he pulled the van into a diner parking lot. They had breakfast and when they finished he asked Deasia to drive so he could sleep for a few hours.

She got them well into Louisiana before stopping for lunch. The kids had enough of the van, so she insisted they get take-out and find a playground. If they could eat and run around for an hour they would sleep for a few hours.

As they sat on a park bench eating Kentucky Fried Chicken box lunches he finally told her they needed to get to Atlanta. They would be there for a few days and then they would be heading back to New Jersey.

Deasia gasped. "We're going home?" "Yes."

As relieved as she was she was also terrified. There was no doubt she would have to face DJ and he was going to be pissed! Then there were her parents, her sister and of course Magda. She decided to call Ang once they were back on the road.

I-10 was closed through most of Louisiana, so they had to take back roads that seemed to go on forever. The kids slept through the state.

In Mississippi I-10 reopened so they cruised through the state. The kids acted up again as they drove through Alabama, but Raffa refused to stop until they entered Georgia. There was no way she could make a phone call with the kids freaking out. She decided to wait until they got to wherever they were going.

By late afternoon they were stretching out on two queen beds at a Holiday Inn in Atlanta, waiting on room service.

Chapter 19:
Camden by the Sea

Jimmy grabbed a couple of beers from the fridge. He wanted to talk with DJ and stress how dangerous it was for him to be walking around the city, especially by himself. Ezee joined them and did his best to change the subject before the conversation got heated.

The cop, Puerto Rican contractor and Black maintenance man reminisced about each of their unique stories and how they ended up living and working in Atlantic City.

"Between 1978 and 2006 were the heydays man," Ezee started. "This city offered a plethora of jobs with middle to upper class salaries," Jimmy added, "The need to fill those jobs caused a mass migration of tens of thousands of immigrant workers. Most of them from the middle east."

"Bush started that crap." DJ said. "Yes, he did during the Gulf War; but it drastically increased under President Obama," Jimmy started, Immigrants fled their war-torn countries and arrived here in the United States with little or no paperwork," Jimmy continued, "Large groups settled in Atlantic City. Most were good people, grateful to have a safe place to raise their children and employment security. Then there were those that took advantage of government programs and worse yet those that took advantage of their own people. They would use people with good credit to apply for mortgages. Once properties were bought they flipped them to members of their community for three times the price the property was worth." DJ looked surprised. "This true?" He asked Ezee. "Yep, many are involved in more traditional crimes like drug dealing, theft and dealing in stolen goods. When the economy took that deep dive in 2008, the crime in Atlantic City escalated. This city was once lit by the brilliant lights of world-famous casinos and was nicknamed the *World's Favorite Playground,* now its nickname is *Camden by the Sea.*"

"I'm offended. I come from Camden," DJ said. Jimmy and Ezee looked at him, surprised. "Really?" Jimmy asked, "I'm originally from across the river in Philadelphia. Did you know Camden was founded a full year before Philadelphia? Camden's growth was slower because the British held the territory and Quakers settled in the area," we studied stuff like this when I was in school. Your generation has no idea." He said looking at DJ

"I didn't have any Quakers for neighbors, that's a fact. I had hood rats for neighbors. Maybe the British should have stayed." DJ said laughing.

"Seriously DJ Camden has so much history. It's a damned shame what happened to the place. Expansion started happening after the Civil War when a steel pen company built its factory in Camden and was followed by the Campbell Soup Company and then the Radio Corporation of America (RCA). Shipbuilding was set up and flourished on the waterfront. When World War II ended industrial factories started closing or leaving the city. Workers moved out to the suburbs or bought farmland. That's when the turn started happening. By the early 1990's half the residents of the city were under the age of twenty-one, African American or Hispanic and the unemployment rate was double the state average. Half of the city's residents lived below the poverty line."

"The murder capitol, of the world sounds more like the Camden I grew up in," DJ said, "My Mom was commuting the hour to and from the casino, and I was home on my own. When I started getting in trouble she said that's it, we're going to A.C. The neighborhoods and schools are much better, and she thought if she cut out her two-hour daily drive time she'd be home to keep me in line. Little did she know we would end up in Camden by the Sea.

"That sucks," Ezee laughed.

Sadly, the chance of becoming the victim of a violent crime in Camden is 1 in 62. The percentage in the rest of the state is 1 in 481.

Becoming a violent crime victim in Atlantic City is 1-137.

Because of its history of corruption and crime, Atlantic City is often referenced as Camden by the Sea. The tale of these two cities that once glimmered with the bright lights of casinos and prosperous, innovative industry with both cities steeped in American history is a sad one.

"Yeah and here we are once again, as it's continued to happen throughout Atlantic City's and Camden's history, infected with the cancer of corruption that breeds out of control crime rates that results in the shuttering of businesses and causes the rapid decaying of both cities." Jimmy added.

"It's the fucking politicians," Ezee raised his voice a bit, "They're forever touting how their ideas will lower the crime rates in our cities. What happens in real life is those politicians take office, small groups of people make a lot of money and move on, those politicians are voted out, others voted in, and the lousy cycle continues."

"Counting on politicians is a losing proposition for sure," Jimmy said, "It's the residents, the people themselves that are the only ones capable of making any remarkable differences. Sadly, that only happens when things get so rotten that they feel they have no other choice than to fight back, even burn it down."

One thing Camden has going for it is after community outrage over police brutality and the increasing violent crimes the residents demanded action. The result was they broke the police union, and the department was torn apart and rebuilt from the bottom up on the premise of community policing. The force doubled in size. As a result, the community and the police have a better relationship, which is positive, but the new officers they hired are unqualified and poorly trained and the crime rate continues ticking upward.

"Let me ask you a question," Jimmy said, "What the hell does DJ stand for?" DJ looked at him, and then turned towards Ezee, "It stands for the name my mother liked for me, so it's DJ to all you'll fuckers."

~

Back in the Middle East the organization's investigation in Africa and Ukraine wrapped up. Leaders made the decision to send a high-ranking investigator to the United States to find and eliminate the dog who dared to steal from them, humiliating the entire organization.

This investigator was chosen carefully. He became a naturalized citizen of the United States under the Bush administration. This would enable him to get through customs without any issues.

Samid Naser first came to the United States in 1999 to attend Washington College in Maryland. He was also on a secret mission to research areas of the country that might be vulnerable to large scale attacks. Consistently sending quality intelligence back to his handlers Samid lived up to the meaning of his name, firm, steadfast and unfaltering. He quickly caught the attention of the organization's leaders.

Going back many generations there's history of Middle Eastern students studying in the United States.

Since 2000, the number of students from the Middle East and North Africa has more than tripled.

After the September 11th attacks, President Bush signed an executive order expediting naturalization for anyone serving in the United States Military. There was a great need for access to people that spoke middle eastern languages as well as English.

Samid entered the United States Military as an interpreter. More importantly at the same time he was supplying oversight for the organizations cell leaders in the States. His investigative skills were second to none.

In 2008 President Bush implemented MAVNI, the Military Accessions Vital to the National Interest. This special program was created to recruit immigrants with specific skills to the U.S. Military.

The Obama Administration expanded MAVNI to include DACA (Deferred Action for Childhood Arrivals) recipients.

During the 2013-2014 school year Saudi Arabia sent more than 54,000 students to Universities in the U.S. That same year Middle Eastern and North African students in the States grew by 20%.

Under President Trump the Pentagon has effectively frozen the program after several terrorist attacks, from the inside on U.S. Military bases.

~

Samid landed at the Newark Airport and as expected had no trouble making his way through customs. A driver, also hand chosen by organization leaders for his loyalty, caution, and thoroughness. The driver placed Samid's luggage in the back and maneuvered the large black SUV out of the parking garage and onto the highway.

"What is the size of the team you put together for me? Are they prepared?" Samid asked the driver. "Since the downturn of the casino industry we haven't had that many of our brothers coming to Atlantic

City but in this case, we have more than we need. The government in this city gives us all the paperwork we need for visas to keep our people here and working. We even have some of our own people working in the government, we control the Democratic Party. The Governor is 100% pro sanctuary State. He refuses to cooperate with the federal government when it comes to immigration."

"This is all good but for this situation I'll need a few men that have no paper trail so they can be burnt. We'll need a handful of illegals that haven't received their new identities, yet. We'll need at least six of them."

"Not a problem," The driver started, "We house and control many illegals."

"I need them to take out a dog that thought he could get away with stealing from us, as well as anyone and everyone that assisted him. It must happen in a public way. Once it's finished, the squad must be eliminated."

"No worries Commander. Who is this thief?"

"I'm not sure, yet. Some funds were picked up or are scheduled to be picked up in New Jersey. I'll need a list of all requests for money from these locations." Samid said as he handed the driver a list. The driver placed the list inside the console.

The driver pulled off into the parking lot of a rest area. He took the list out and made a phone call.

"The lists will be ready for you shortly." The driver assured Samid.

Pulling up to the front entrance of a casino, the driver got out and went around to open the door for the investigator. As the two men approached the front door the driver showed the doorman a key card.

The doorman welcomed Samid and told him his luggage would be taken to his suite.

The driver spoke with a young woman behind the counter. The woman handed him comps for the casino's high- end restaurant.

As Samid and the driver ate, a man asked to join them at their table. Speaking in their language he handed Samid $100,000 in vouchers and told him to enjoy the tables during his stay.

"Do they need to be used here, at this casino?" Samid asked. "Of course, yes they are only good here."

When they finished eating the driver excused himself and Samid made his way to his suite.

Early the next morning the driver returned to the casino with the list of money pick-up locations the Commander asked.

Chapter 20:
48 Blocks

The driver explained to the investigator how he divided the list into three groups based on location. The first group was three stores in the suburbs outside of Atlantic City. The second group was only one store in Newark, New Jersey and the last group was ten stores, all found in Atlantic City.

Surprised at how many locations were within the forty-eight blocks of Atlantic City, the investigator told the driver, "Excellent work. You're dominating this place."

"I suggest we start with the location that is the furthest from here, Newark," The driver explained, "The store in Newark isn't as busy with these types of transactions so the owner may be able to remember more details about our mark. The other stores handle hundreds of transactions each day."

The store in Newark was fruitless.

Next they visited a gas station that also housed a convenience store. They met with the manager who greeted them and then escorted them to the back office where they met with the owner. The investigator explained they were looking for a Black man whose transaction resulted in him receiving $4000.

Most customers fit that description but the amount, $4000 isn't an amount we see often. He opens his desk drawer and hands the driver a stack of recent receipts. While the investigator and the driver go through them, the store owner prepared three cups of tea.

Not one $4000 receipt was found but they did discover there was one pending. The owner was instructed to notify the driver immediately when the man showed up to collect. “Keep him here for as long as you can. If he leaves make sure you get a description of him and his vehicle including the license plate number. Do not disappoint me.” Samid said causing the owner to shudder.

The same scenario played out at the next two County stores.

At the first store in Atlantic City the store manager said, “The description is too vague. It describes most of our customers.” The investigator became agitated and stormed out of the store. The driver gave the manager his business card and instructed him to call the instant anyone came in for $4000.

When they arrived at the Seven-Eleven the manager told them, “Yes, one of my regulars was in here yesterday. He claimed he was picking up for his boss, a Jew.” The investigator tensed.

“This guy has a lot of trouble. His wife messes with a gang, MS13 and they’ve threatened him many times.” The manager said.

The investigator instructed him to call immediately if he returns. As the two men left the store, the manager realized he’d been to a picnic across the street from DJ’s house and he knew his address.

“We’ll be back tomorrow to look through your security tapes and receipts.” The driver said.

~

The vibe in Atlantic City shifts with the weather. With May comes the best kind of vibe, usually. This May was different. Jimmy couldn’t shake the feeling that the other shoe was about to drop, a big shoe.

After spending most of the morning at big box stores picking up items for the business and the house, he needed a pick me up. First he pulled up to a corner store. As a cop he befriended the owner, and even helped him several times over the years. He decided to stop in and say hello.

The store owner appeared anxious. “Did you get robbed?” Jimmy asked him. The man looked around to make sure his employees and the few customers in the store where out of ear shot. “No not robbed. It’s been crazy though. I heard there are some bad people arriving in town, dangerous people. No one seems to know why.” Curious, Jimmy tells him, “Please call if you need anything and be careful.”

His body tensed and Jimmy knew what that meant. Some serious shit was about to go down. He walked back towards his car but instead decided to cross the street and go into the Seven-Eleven where DJ and him often stopped for coffee.

As he poured his coffee he couldn’t help overhearing the manager and another man at the register having a conversation in Arabic. To the left of the front door was another man, standing there, watching the other two men talk.

“The conversation sounds heated.” Jimmy thought. When Jimmy approached the register, the manager walked the other man towards the back of the store and opened the door leading to the office. Once the man was in the office the store manager hustled back to his position behind the register. He greeted the cop. “Everything okay?” Jimmy asked as he nodded towards the back room. “Yes, yes Jimmy. Everything’s good. It’s a new regional manager.

Jimmy knew that wasn’t true and he figured it had something to do with the dangerous people in town. The manager didn’t charge him for his coffee and said, “Have a good day my friend.”

Jimmy walked across the street to his car and drove back to the Seven-Eleven. He sat there, with an unobstructed view into the store and sipped his coffee. Ten minutes later the manager walked out of the store with the investigator. Jimmy did his best to read their lips, but they were speaking in their language. He nearly spilled his coffee when the manager clearly said, Davis and went on to give the man DJ's old address. "What's that idiot gotten himself into?"

Jimmy followed them to the casino. "This is the dangerous guy from out of town." Jimmy was sure.

~

The driver arranged a meeting with the squad. The squad was given instructions to go to the address and to take care of everyone in the house.

~

That night under the cover of darkness a five- man team surrounded the house DJ shared with his wife and kids. As the investigator and driver stood watch out front the team entered the home. DJ's cousin, his girlfriend and their two small children were stabbed while they slept. The squad trashed the house, took pictures of the victims and spray painted MS13 symbols on the walls, as instructed and they fled.

Ezee happened to glance over at his security monitor. Not believing what he was seeing he looked closer. He dialed Jimmy's number. "We got trouble. Big trouble. I'm watching a bunch of guys, all in dark clothes, scarves on their heads and faces surrounding DJ's house. Is he at the warehouse?" "Yeah he is. Hang on," Jimmy said as he dialed the private dispatch number for 911 and told them what was happening, "Are you and your family okay Ezee?" "Yeah Jim we're okay. I'm watching as they pull away now. I got a good plate number and I'm texting you a shot of the two that were standing out front."

Jimmy clicked on the text and immediately recognized the guy as the so- called new area manager for Seven-Eleven.

The first patrol car arrived.

Jimmy arrived at Ezee's house to get a better look at the security footage. There was no doubt in his mind, it was the same guy he saw at the Seven-Eleven that afternoon.

Within minutes of discovering the gruesome scene inside the house sirens could be heard in the distance. The street quickly filled with emergency vehicles.

Jimmy left and went to the warehouse to make sure they hadn't found DJ.

Ezee 's house filled with detectives that wanted to view the video.

DJ was sound asleep. Jimmy woke him up and told him what happened.

"Is my cuz and his family okay?" "I'm not sure." Jimmy answered.

"Listen DJ I don't know who you pissed- off while you were away or who knows while you've been here, but they want you and they aren't about to give up. You cannot leave this building, and no one can know you are here. No going for coffee, for money, to get laid, nothing. Stay put until we can figure out a way to stop this. And remember, if someone gets in here do whatever you have to do to get up there." Jimmy explained while pointing to the ceiling. He went on to explain to him where he hid the bricks in the rafters. "If you drop one don't miss!"

~

Early the next morning the investigator and the driver went back to the Seven-Eleven and went through that week's security videos. When the manager pointed out DJ the driver and the investigator knew at once the squad killed the wrong guy the night before.

"Why did you give us the wrong address? They demanded of the manager. "He must have moved. I was there, at his house less than a month ago." When the investigator heard the manager say he was at the house of the man they were searching for he assumed they were friends, and he became furious.

"Where is he living now?" He shouted. The manager rattled off three other locations DJ may frequent. Out of character, the investigator pulled out a gun and shot the manager.

Samid was well known for his patience and his diligence. This assignment was spiraling out of control. He feared his anger for this man, this infidel was clouding his judgement and that made him angrier.

"Let's Go." He barked to the driver.

A few minutes later two police detectives arrived to look at the previous days video footage. They were acting on the information Jimmy gave them the night before. What they discovered was a fifth victim, the store manager. The video security footage was missing.

~

The driver was getting more nervous that his own life, and the life of his family was in jeopardy. He became desperate for information. Farah, the Syrian wife of one of the men they had managing rental properties for the organization worked at City Hall.

He called her at work and asked her to run the name of the last tenant. Ten minutes later she returned his call and informed him that the man was recently divorced. She gave him the address they had on file and told him that was the address they sent priority mail to and that it needed to be signed for by whoever answered the door. The receipt from the post office, in her file was signed by DJ Davis.

The investigator was impressed at first. It didn't last. "Why didn't you call her first you idiot? LET'S GO!" He yelled.

Not expecting the address given to them to belong to a commercial building, the investigator demanded at least three more men. "Untraceable men, remember!"

They were confused. Was this where he worked, or lived?

Within an hour and following orders, the squad of eight spread their vehicles out on the block. They had the warehouse surrounded.

There was no sign of the man they were looking for coming or going so they waited, impatiently.

Chapter 21:
Crossfire

Jimmy was scheduled to go to the shooting range with a group of retired cops, one of them being his longtime partner, Steve. To keep their weapons certifications for federal, conceal and carry permits up to date they were evaluated twice a year. Today was practice day for that test. Steve offered to drive, so the plan was for everyone to meet at Jimmy's shop, and they would drive to the range together, in Steve's SUV.

Jimmy had an appointment with a customer but figured he'd be back at the shop before the guys arrived. The home- owner was undecided on the layout for her new kitchen so it was taking longer than he expected. Knowing his friends would be arriving soon to pick him up, he made a quick call to the shop. His sales rep answered. He told her, "A few guys may stop in looking for me, tell them I'm running late."

~

Growing more frustrated the investigator got out of the SUV against his driver's advice. He slammed the door and brazenly walked into the shop. He told the sales rep he was looking for custom cabinets for a vacation home he recently bought on the beach side. He followed her to a wall of custom cabinet door samples. She told him to take his time looking them over and she went back to her desk to answer another phone call.

It was getting close to closing time. DJ walked through the fabrication area and then through the showroom. He was waiting for Jimmy to return, hoping he had news on his cousin's killers.

Haunted by the thought of his cousin's girlfriend and their innocent little boy and baby girl killed so brutally and devastated by the loss of his cousin DJ couldn't sleep.

His grief and anger came in alternating waves, one after the other. "What kind of people take out little babies like that?" He whispered to himself.

He picked up his phone and scrolled through the news feed. Local Atlantic City sources were reporting that MS13 was responsible. "I'm responsible," he mumbled to himself, choking back tears, "She's responsible! This is more on her, than on me!"

This confirmed for him that all of this was indeed his wife's fault. The thought that his kids were with them was horrifying. He continued struggling with the decision to report them missing or not. It was clear as day that they didn't value the lives of kids, so now he was leaning strongly towards making that report. He was seriously considering filing kidnapping charges against Deasia too. He planned to ask for Jimmy's advice on the best way to go about it.

His biggest fear was, if he filed the kidnapping charges, was that Raffa would take it out on his kids. His gut was telling him to hold off until he could be sure they wouldn't be harmed. He missed them so much.

As he walked by the investigator DJ was sure the man was staring at him. As he passed him he turned, stared back at the stranger, "Excuse me do I know you?" The investigator said, "You get your coffee at the Seven-Eleven." "Yeah that's right, do you work there? I don't recognize you," DJ said with of twinge of sarcasm. Immediately he regretted answering the man at all. Turning towards him, DJ held his hand out and shook the man's hand briskly before quickly making his way back through the fabrication room and into his makeshift bedroom.

Lying on his bed he put his pillow over his face and sobbed. "What have I done?"

The sales rep rejoined Samid at the cabinet display and directed him towards the counter display that was set up on the other side of the showroom. She explained the difference between granite, quartz, marble, and the newest types of laminate and Corian to him.

She was getting the distinct feeling the guy wasn't all that interested in cabinets. Instead, he was looking over her shoulder towards the door that led to the fabrication area. Trying her best to get him to focus on remodeling his kitchen, she asked "Do you have kids? They must be excited about the new beach house."

He wasn't impressed by her, or any woman in the disgusting Country, especially the women that held positions of power and those that were educated. "What a waste." He muttered under his breath. "She has this stupid job and thinks she's smarter than me."

As Jimmy drove down the street heading towards his warehouse he couldn't help noticing a dark colored SUVs in front of his shop and another one in the small parking lot, on the left side of the building. He rode slowly around the block and saw another one. It was impossible to miss them. Let's say they aren't the usual neighborhood vehicles. Two men, wearing Keffiyehs stood outside the vehicle smoking cigarettes.

"What the hell is going on?" Jimmy wondered. His adrenalin kicked into high gear. Either there was a high- level celebrity in town or he had trouble. Serious trouble.

He called Steve, hoping he was already at the warehouse. "I got a problem." "I see. We're rolling up to your shop and wondering if you're having a terrorist convention." Steve answered, his adrenaline kicking in too.

"This is no joke. Gear up, watch the numbers and stand by for a plan." Jimmy clicked off the call and dialed Frank, the FBI agent. "MS13 after your buddy again?" Frank asked. "Yep I think they found DJ" Are you still in that Homeland Security detail? These guys are wearing head covers. They ain't gang bangers. I'm about to be hit. I got a fight on my hands. You need to call for the Homeland Rapid Response Team. Bring all the heat or I'm gonna be fucked!" "I was afraid this was much darker than we thought," Frank said. I'll call my field office for back-up. I'm in the neighborhood so I'll be right there. Be careful Jim."

Jimmy pulled into the parking lot and pulled up on an angle as close to the SUV as possible, making it difficult for that vehicle to back out. Noticing Steve's blue pick-up truck coming up the street Jimmy was relieved. He also recognized Frank's Ford pulling up on the side street to the right. "That was fast!" Jimmy said aloud to himself. He knew he would have plenty of immediate back-up if needed.

He walked into the shop. Immediately he recognized the guy standing with his sales rep. Those black eyes and that thick unibrow were hard to forget. Wanting to first make sure DJ was okay he walked through the showroom and made his way into the fabrication area and then into DJ's room.

"What am I gonna do about these gangbangers?" DJ pleaded., "I messed up so bad." "I'm positive this is not MS13 DJ," Jimmy answered, "You interfered with some sort of serious shit on a global scale. You had to go after that damned money didn't you! There were so many better ways to manage your situation. Right now, we need to keep you alive. Get up into the rafters and be quiet, NOW!"

The look in Jimmy's eyes was all he needed to know something awful was about to happen. As quickly as he could move he climbed up metal storage shelves that were mounted to the wall. His leg was still broken but he had to take the brace off to climb. Standing on the top shelf he reached up for a steel beam and shimmied himself up into rafters. Noticing little piles of bricks as he crawled along the narrow wooden boards and not knowing Jimmy strategically placed them he thought, “That’s weird.” He made his way to a dark corner that allowed him to see down into the showroom and the fabrication area without anyone seeing him from below.

Jimmy walked back into the fabrication area and quietly told each member of his crew to call it a night. It was closing time anyway, so no one questioned him. Following the last of his employees to the front door, he stood there by the door waiting for the last few customers to leave.

Of all days, this was one of the busiest he’d had in quite a while. If it weren’t for the crowd DJ would already be dead.

The investigator realized the shop was about to close. He told the sales rep he was going to bring his wife in the following day. He hurried out and as soon as the driver saw him in the doorway he pulled up, jumped out and opened the back door on the passenger side of the vehicle. “The dog is inside the building!” Once his Commander was safely in the car, they sped off.

“Damn;” Jimmy thought to himself, “Who the hell is that guy?” He grabbed a piece of paper from the sales area and jotted down the license plate number. He texted the number to Frank and Steve.

~

The investigator ordered the squad to immediately storm the building. “Under no circumstances are you to let that thief get away, kill them all or else!”

On high alert, the assassins took a good look at the photos they were given of DJ. There was no way they wanted to chance killing the wrong guy again.

The driver took the fastest route he knew to the casino. He dropped the investigator off at the front door to pack and then he drove back towards the warehouse. Pulling onto a side street, where he had a view of the front door, he sat and watched as his squad was slowly making their way towards the building.

Back at the casino Samid made his way to a private poker table where he sat down and requested a water.

~

The text alert on Jimmy's phone startled him. *Four actors walking by side door and four headed to the front door. Terrorist meeting about to begin. All four of us are locked and loaded.*

Steve parked blocking the parking lot exit and Frank pulled up in front of the shop beside another SUV, blocking it in.

"What timing," Jimmy thought, "Terrorist decided to hit us on the same day I have my own squad here. Looking up Jimmy said loud to the patron saint of police officers, "Thank you Saint Michael! It couldn't be more perfect."

He sent a group text. *Whatever you do don't shoot the Black guy in the rafters. He's their mark. I set up a kill zone in between the fabrication shop and the showroom. I'm in the showroom. Try to funnel them in and keep me posted on the numbers, let me know how many as they enter.*

There was a full kitchen display set up a few feet from the front entrance. Jimmy climbed into a cabinet under the center island. There were two Beretta's taped to the top of the inside of the cabinet. Jimmy tucked one into the back of his waistband and held the other.

All eight in the building. Steve and the other three retired cops tactically entered one by one through the side door. Jimmy strained to decide from which direction footsteps were coming.

He was able to peer out through the front and the back of the cabinet.

He watched as Steve cocked his gun and climbed into a tall broom cabinet. Looking back towards the front, three men slowly entered through the front door.

The three other retired cops quickly scattered across the work area and found machinery or cabinets to crouch behind.

Looking out through the front Jimmy saw two men four feet from his hiding place, while a third made his way to the back of the room. He pushed open the cabinet doors as hard and loudly as he could and at once shot the two assassins in front of him. As he threw himself back into the cabinet the third guy tried shooting down at him, but the bullets deflected off the granite countertop. Knowing he only had seconds before the guy would shoot again through the back of the cabinet, Jimmy crouched on his hands and knees and tried to lift the granite top off its cabinet base with his back. It took three tries before he busted the seal holding the counter in place and sent the solid stone flying, through the air while screaming, "PUSH to let all the good guys know it was on!" Eight-hundred pounds of granite landed on the third assassin's feet. He screamed in agony but managed to clumsily aim his weapon at Jimmy, who was able to shoot first.

Another assassin jumped on Jimmy's back sending his weapon sliding across the concrete floor. He felt an all too familiar sharp pain down his left leg and knew he fucked his back up again. Gasping for every ounce of adrenalin he could muster he held the guy's right wrist tight, trying to stop the blood flow to his hand with the hope he'd drop the assault rifle he had a death grip on. The two battled hand to hand for a few seconds that seemed like an hour. Looking to his left, praying for some backup he saw Steve with one arm around a terrorist's neck while he tried to disarm him with the other arm. The bastard broke away and aimed at Steve, but Steve shot first.

Steve made his way over to Jimmy who finally managed to shoot his assailant.

Hearing shots rapidly fired outside the building Jimmy and Steve assumed some of the actors fled and were being confronted by Frank. Slightly relieved, they kept moving.

Jimmy slowly made his way towards the fabrication area. He looked up and caught a glimpse of DJ in the rafters. With his hand he signaled to him to keep his head down. What he missed was DJ trying to warn him.

DJ could not believe what he was seeing below. He was struggling to imagine a scenario where they all made it out of the building alive.

In the doorway to the fabrication area, Jimmy peered slowly to the right and there was a guy with a gun pointed at his face. Hoping Steve and Frank were right behind and wanting to give them a clear shot at the bad guy, Jimmy moved ever so slightly to the left. "Where is he?" The assassin demanded. "Who?" Jimmy asked. "We know he's here. The Black man. We have this building surrounded. Give him up NOW!"

Carefully Jimmy slid even further to the left as three bricks fell from the rafters. Two of them hit the terrorist in the back of the head. He fell forward with a loud thud. He looked up at DJ and gave him a thumbs up.

One of the retired cops held up two fingers, signaling to Jimmy that there were still two more in the building. With all the good guys now safely out of the fabrication area and in the showroom Jimmy signaled to the fabrication door. Steve and the other retired cops started firing a nonstop stream of bullets at the fabrication door. This was a distraction tactic they hoped would encourage the last two bad actors to make a run for the front door. It worked like a charm.

Both men were at once taken down by Frank as they ran through the front door shooting at him.

With all the terrorists now accounted for the cops entered the building.

~

The driver who saw four members of his squad taken down in front of the warehouse feared the worst when the other four members didn't come out of the building. The only good thought he could summon was he didn't have to kill the squad, the cops did it for him.

How would he find out if the thief was finished off? No squad members were answering his calls or his texts. Were all his men dead or where there a few in custody? Hearing sirens in the distance he realized he was a sitting duck and knew he had to get out of there fast.

He called his wife and told her to get the kids and get out of the house immediately. She insisted on asking questions, so he shouted at her. "GO NOW!" Then he texted Samid. *It's done. We must go quickly. Meet you out front of the casino as soon as I change vehicles.*

The driver backed the SUV into his garage. He took the keys to his marked cab, a mini- van from a hook on the wall. He worked as a cab driver and sometimes had an associate drive one of his vehicles.

The law would be stopping all dark colored SUVs, so this was his best move.

~

Frank took control of the scene inside the warehouse and out. He instructed everyone to find a seat and to stay put while they waited for forensics.

Jimmy was sick to his stomach, realizing it was all far from over. They had no idea how many more assassins were in town or how many more could be summoned. Then there was the threat of MS13 still out there waiting for an opportunity to take another shot at DJ and whoever got in their way. He looked around at the destruction in his shop and then focused on the forensics team as they methodically did their job.

"There's a driver and a boss out there somewhere," Jimmy said, "Did you get the plate number I texted you?" "It came back as an A.C. cab driver. We have agents at the courthouse pulling cab licenses now. Hopefully, we'll have photos for you to look at shortly."

Jimmy grimaced but refused to give in to the constant pain in his back. He opened a drawer in the sales area and pulled out a bottle of Motrin and quickly swallowed four with a gulp of coffee from a cup he left on the counter that morning.

~

Once Samid was in the back seat the driver intentionally lied to his Commander. He fabricated a story that involved him taking DJ down on his own. "The squad was in the building cleaning up when the cops entered and boxed them in. They were all killed." Reasoning with himself he thought that once they were on a plane and out of the country, Samid would put this assignment far behind him and start plotting his next investigation.

As they approached the bridge that would take them across the river into New York, Samid told the driver to pull into the rest area.

The driver stood watch just inside the men's room door. Enemies of the Commander could be anywhere so if anyone tried to enter he told them that rest room was being cleaned and would only be a few minutes.

Quietly a man approached the driver from behind and slit his throat.

Samid spit on the driver as he stepped over the bloody mess. He and his new driver made their way through the crowded lobby towards the exit. As they pushed opened the door they heard screams coming from the area of the rest room. They hustled into a sedan and headed over the bridge into New York.

Two hours later Samid was in a first- class window seat, in the air headed to London. He chose London as a precaution. Authorities may have been tracking flights departing for the middle east.

While he was impressed with the vast numbers of the New Jersey organization, Samid was deeply disappointed in the leadership. They were supposed to be highly trained and able to manage anything. Taking out one infidel shouldn't have been as difficult as it was. Changes would have to be made and quickly if they were going to continue growing their dominance in the area.

~

Frank, along with a homeland security officer, and an IRS agent questioned DJ relentlessly for hours. When the IRS agent said for the third time, "You are going to end up in jail for illegally bringing money into the United States," DJ became visibly upset. Jimmy couldn't stand to watch anymore and insisted they all let the guy get some rest.

As he walked DJ back to his room, the IRS agent called out, "Donald, we are not done. I'll need more information tomorrow."

"Donald! Jimmy turned and looked at him with a curious look. You've got to be kidding me!" Jimmy couldn't help himself, he laughed hysterically. "Fuck off," DJ said. "Seriously that's your name?" Jimmy said trying not to laugh. "My mother worked for Trump. She started as a cashier in his casino. She worked her way up to public relations and became an account manager. Her respect for him was, still is off the charts. Out of respect for him she named me Donald John. When I was a kid she was always saying, he's going to run for President one day. My Mama was right, Donald Trump ran for President and won!" "That's wild." Jimmy said. "I guess he wasn't racist before he was President?" Jimmy laughed again. "Fuck off." DJ said under his breath.

"That was a cool move." DJ said pointing to the door as they walked through the fabrication room. How'd you all know what each other was thinking? You'll were like superheroes the way you just started shooting in sync! That door is destroyed" "It's called a plan," Jimmy answered. "You are one bad ass hero man." DJ answered.

Jimmy thought for a minute and then said, "I served, I sacrificed, I regret nothing. I'm not a hero. I'm a retired police officer and my service has no expiration date. Feeling himself getting emotional Jimmy changed the subject. "Look at my damned shop. A lot more than that door got destroyed." "I'll give you $4000 towards the repairs." DJ said. Jimmy laughed. "I think it's gonna take a lot more than that to clean up this mess. We'll worry about all that later."

DJ sat down on his cot. "I can't believe I gotta go to jail. This is some seriously fucked up shit!. How about that racist IRS dude?" DJ started to rant, "Can you believe they won't even let me get the rest of the money? I can't believe I told them there was more. How am I supposed to pay a decent attorney now? They're gonna figure out where all that money came from, confiscate it, and use it to chase some poor brothers for running drugs. The government is always looking for ways to set up some Black dude. That IRS dude told me if I try to collect the money, they'll charge me with interfering with a federal investigation. How long do you think I gotta go to jail for? I need to find my kids and get them away from those gang bangers. They killed my cousin and his family."

"That wasn't the gang DJ," Jimmy said angrily, "That was terrorists! Middle Eastern terrorists! Do you get how fucking serious this is? Do you even realize how many lives were in danger today? This is your problem DJ You hate the people that put their own lives on the line to save your sorry ass. You do get that your life was saved, right? You need to do some serious work on that stinking rotten thinking of yours." "I'm really not the bad guy here," DJ answered, "I'm the victim. They stole from me. I was only trying to fight back, to get what was rightfully mine." "I get that but there's a process and sometimes it actually works for the good guys." Jimmy answered.

I don't think they'll convict you of anything DJ. Please be chill and play along with the game. For right now, lay down for a while.

Jimmy was exhausted, and his mind was racing not to mention the intense pain running down his leg. He had to keep it together a little bit longer. They needed him to pick out the driver from a photo line-up.

Maria was either calling or texting every five-minutes all night wanting to make sure her husband was okay and wanting to know what she could do to help. Jimmy asked her to have coffee and donuts delivered.

Reporters were calling on the shop phone. Jimmy was told directly by his superiors not to give any comments, yet. The departments would get together and have their spokespeople craft a press release. "That will no doubt be total bullshit." Jimmy thought.

He looked around at the destruction and the lost lives. Frank noticed and said, "It was either them or us, no doubt about that."

Steve added, "Good plan."

It was dawn before the forensics team gave the okay for the bodies to be removed from the warehouse.

They woke DJ and removed him too, in handcuffs. Jimmy said, "Keep your shit together. It's for the best. Jail is the safest place for you to be right now, seriously. I'll get you outta there as soon as it's safe."

DJ in shock, was unable to process anything that happened over the last three days. He could only think about wanting to go to sleep, wanting it to all go away. The cot in his jail cell wasn't much different than the one he'd been sleeping on in the storage closet. He fell into a deep sleep.

Jimmy identified the driver and a BOLO (be on the lookout) was broadcast for him.

As fellow officers were driving him home, he looked at all the missed calls he had. He decided to call Ezee back. Ezee said, "Dude what the fuck happened it's all over the news. Your shop is covered with police tape, and they were pulling dead bodies out in bags." Jimmy told him everyone was safe and after telling him what had happen, Ezee said, "That's fucked up!" Jimmy said, "Not as Fucked up as DJ's real name." Ezee said, "you know what his real name is!" Jimmy said, "Yea, he's named after our favorite president." Ezee said, "No Fucking Way!" Jimmy said, "Yep, his mom just loved Donald John Trump so much for all the opportunities she was provided when working at Trump Plaza she named her kid after him." Ezee said, "No wonder the guy is so angry." They both laughed and said they would catch up the next day.

Once home and his front door was shut and locked, Jimmy felt the last bit of adrenaline leave his body and exhaustion took its place.

He would have to trust the officer in the unmarked car out front to keep his family and him safe, for now.

Chapter 22:
Fallout

DJ's arraignment was the following Monday. He'd spent the weekend in the Atlantic City Police Department's jail. If he was being honest it wasn't that bad. He slept most of the weekend. When he wasn't asleep cops on duty stopped by his cell to chat. He felt like a celebrity.

They were fascinated with him and wanted to hear every detail of his story and he was in his glory with all the attention. They couldn't believe how he stung a terrorist organization, got away with it, and lived to talk about it, so far.

Sitting behind him in court was Jimmy, Ezee, Frank and Steve. For the first time in his life, he felt supported and confident. It was an odd feeling for him, the support by a bunch of law enforcement pricks.

He hoped they could keep him out of prison. He knew for sure he wouldn't do well in an actual prison.

He'd been thinking seriously about what Jimmy told him at the shop. If he was being honest, his thinking has been off for most of his life. He knew it was time to dig deep for some humility and gratefulness.

When Judge Hart walked into the courtroom and took her place at the bench, DJ's heart sank. He couldn't decide whether she was good news or unwelcome news. She did approve his divorce and give him custody of his kids but her words warning him to stay out of trouble were harsh. He wondered if she knew he lost the kids. His stomach was in knots. This woman had the power to lock him up for twenty-years.

Judge Hart started the hearing off dropping an extensive list of charges. Then she lectured him for twenty-minutes on the importance of thinking things thoroughly through and not being stupid. Yes, she called him stupid at least three times. Each time DJ slumped lower in his seat.

When all was said and done, the judge ordered him to be remanded in the police station jail for two weeks for not reporting a crime.

DJ put his face in his hands and cried. He was relieved. They were all relieved.

Patting him on the back, Frank said, "Don't worry DJ we'll do our best to get you outta that place sooner, as long as it's safe."

Once he was back in his cell, he asked the cop on duty to help him file a missing person's report for Deasia and his kid's. He filed kidnapping charges as well and asked the officer to let Frank know.

Frank would now be able to have Deasia and Raffa taken into custody. Keeping track of her whereabouts was finally going to pay off. Her and Raffa had been leading FBI agents to all sorts of MS13 members and criminal activity in other states.

He'd was informed they were in Texas and was surprised to find when he called the agent in Houston that the couple hit the road again. The agent wasn't sure what their destination was only that they were heading east. He promised to keep Frank posted.

~

Fuming over the debacle in New Jersey, Samid laid low at a London safe house. This was most certainly going to affect his reputation. The thought crossed his mind more than a few times that he may meet the same fate as the driver.

He pieced together, on paper everything that happened, from the beginning. He needed to figure out how this happened in the first place. In hindsight, he knew his men should have been ordered to take Donald Davis alive. He should've questioned him, himself. Second guessing himself he also reconsidered whether all those responsible in Africa were taken out. Those in charge at the money exchange businesses were taken out. The African taxi driver was eliminated. "Did he have accomplices? If he did how will I ever find them now?

The Commander relayed to his bosses in Syria that he was in London tying up loose ends.

The last loose end was him. Filled with shame and knowing he would be held accountable by his superiors and knowing what that meant, he said his morning prayers, put his belongings in order and put two knives in his waistband.

He had a cup of tea in the hotel lobby before heading outside to formulate his plan. Noticing four police officers as he entered a small park, his plan became clear. Walking behind a bench, where two women sat reading newspapers, he took both knives out and slit the throat of one woman and stabbed the other in the back of the neck.

Backing up to a jogging path he turned and used both knives to kill a young man. As passersby noticed the women sitting on the bench in pools of blood and began screaming. The cops ran for the park entrance hoping to block whoever the assailant was inside the park.

Samid continued his carnage stabbing to death two more joggers on the path before running back into the center of the park. The cops tried to surround him, demanding he drop the knives. He lunged at them stabbing one of the officers in the arm. Another cop knocked him down and wrestled with the knife only to get stabbed in the chest. As Samid stood up and ran towards the entrance gates yelling Allah Akbar he was shot in the head by an armed officer and fell forward.

His plan to take out as many infidels as possible and dying a martyr instead of a failure in the eyes of his superiors and his country was successful.

~

Jimmy came clean with Maria and finally told her the entire story. She knew from the beginning Jimmy wasn't telling her the full DJ story and she wasn't happy to find out the details, the danger her husband put himself and their family in. It was hard to stay angry while feeling so relieved and realizing that it could have all been so much worse.

Maria and Jimmy met at the police academy where she was the hand-to-hand instructor. He never seemed to remember or give her credit for the tough, accomplished woman she was. She insisted on helping with the clean-up at the shop. He welcomed the help.

"That hand to hand training came in handy babe," he said smiling at her. They both laughed.

Once the police, the FBI and Homeland Security finished collecting evidence and closed the investigation at the warehouse, Ezee helped Jimmy replace the door to the fabrication area and, also helped him repair the bullet holes in the showroom cabinets.

It seemed every time they repaired one they found another.

"I'm sorry I got you involved in all this craziness," He said to Jimmy, "I didn't wanna see the guy get killed. Believe me I had *no idea* it would come to this, that all this would go down." "You were right about the guy Ezee," Jimmy said, "He really isn't that bad of a guy. He does constantly put himself in stupid positions though. Hopefully, this whole thing will help him see that. I can't help but like the guy. And he's named after a President." Ezee shook his head. "I like the President Jimmy, but I do get why DJ would be pissed."

That night Jimmy and Maria were sitting on the sofa in their family room watching cable news. Both were speechless when breaking news came across the screen.

What they already characterized as a terrorist attack in a London Park ended with the police killing the terrorist and six-innocent people dead. Four more innocents were injured. The most shocking part of the story was Jimmy immediately recognized the terrorist.

He called Frank. "I know Jimmy. I was going to call you in the morning once I had more info. Homeland notified me a few minutes ago. Good riddance! Hopefully, they were able to get a read on where he came from and who else was involved. If not we'll continue to follow the money."

~

A few days later Ezee got a call from DJ "They're letting me out early! Can you pick me up?"

Worried about DJ's safety, knowing MS13 was still out there, Ezee called Jimmy.

The two of them decided it would be best if DJ continued to keep a low profile. It was decided he would come back to the shop and stay in his closet.

Finishing his release paperwork took forever, and DJ was not happy about going back to his warehouse jail.

As they left the police station and were walking down the ramp that led to the sidewalk, DJ spotted a low rider and on instinct he pulled Ezee to the ground and threw himself on top of him as shots rang out. The car sped away. "What the fuck!" He yelled! They spent another two hours inside the precinct being questioned by officers and filling out reports.

Figuring the gang bangers were laying low after their failed attempt on his life, DJ asked Ezee and Jimmy to take him to his house. “I’m not sure that’s such a promising idea.” Jimmy responded. “I need to see it,” DJ said, “Sooner or later I need to decide about the place. I’d rather get it over with. Besides, I could hear something about my kids any day now. They need a home.” “They do DJ, but it needs to be safe too.” Jimmy added.

As he put the key in front door and turned the knob DJ was filled with emotion. Would his Auntie ever speak to him again? Would his mom ever forgive him? “My cousin,” He sobbed, “I was only trying to help. Why do I fuck everything up?”

Jimmy and Ezee hugged him and did their best to assure him it wasn’t his fault.

Picking his head up and looking around, DJ realized his house was spotless. Things hadn’t been this put together since before Deasia’s accident. DJ sobbed again, “Who did this?” He asked. “All the ladies in the neighborhood got together and wanted to do something for your family. This is what they came up with,” Ezee said, “They also started a Go Fund Me for you. You got a nice nest egg waiting for you.”

“Why would I ever want to move away from neighbors like this?” DJ answered.

“In the meantime, get what you need and let’s get out of here before the gangbangers crawl back out from under their rocks.” Jimmy said.

Back at the shop, the three of them talked about everything that happened over pizza and beers.

Frank stopped by to let DJ know Deasia was in Texas for a short time and was now on the move again. “My kids, are they okay?” DJ asked. “From what the agents have seen, they appear to be fine.” “Now that you filed those charges, as soon as we can, we'll get those kids back to you."

Jimmy asked Frank what would be happening, would they be involved in any further investigations or hearings. "I'm not sure yet but my guess is there isn't anyone that was physically involved, here left. It depends on what's discovered through the different agency investigations." Frank said.

That night as he laid on the cot, DJ wondered if he should keep his secret from Ezee and Jimmy. Feeling guilty was getting to him. Both men have proven they could be trusted by him, but part of DJ still couldn't be all in with his trust. For now, the secret was his, and his alone.

Remembering what Ezee said about the Go Fund Me page, DJ Googled his name and the words Go Fund Me. He sat straight up and stared at the tiny screen trying to process what he saw. $32,000 was collected to help him and his family.

"What do you know," He said to himself, "This is going to help me get back on my feet." He became emotional again and decided he would give a part to his aunt. It wouldn't bring his cousin, the kids or his cousin's girlfriend back but he hoped it would help her since she'd been unable to work due to her grief.

Chapter 23:
Atlanta

Incessant pounding woke DJ from a sound sleep. "Did Jimmy forget his keys?" He said aloud as he walked towards the shop door. About to push open the door he thought he heard someone speaking *Spanish.* He froze. "Think." He told himself.

Remembering the security cameras Jimmy had installed he quietly made his way to the office area. Each pound on the door caused him to jump. His adrenaline was surging. He clicked on the cameras and gasped.

He ran back to his room, grabbed his phone, and called Jimmy. "I got to run," He whispered, "There's four gang bangers at the door." "You know the drill DJ," Jimmy instructed, "Get up in those rafters. I'm outside and help is on the way. There's a raid happening on MS13 right now and with any luck all your enemies will be behind bars within hours."

~

Deasia thought she was dreaming until her daughter shook her shoulder. Someone was most definitely banging on their hotel room door. "Get the kids in the bathroom now," Raffa ordered as he cocked his pistol and with his back against the wall made his way towards the door, "Now!" He said a bit louder.

She struggled to wake the other two kids and ended up carrying them one at a time into the bathroom. All three kids started to whimper. Deasia shushed them and asked Raffa who was banging on the door. "It's the law." No sooner did he say that when they heard, "Police, open the door now." The hotel phone on the nightstand was ringing. Deasia walked towards it and Raffa yelled, "Don't answer that phone." Ignoring him Deasia picked up the phone. It was a female FBI agent. She asked Deasia where the kids were and then asked her if she had a weapon. "No of course not," Deasia answered shaking. The agent instructed her to go into the bathroom and to stay there.

As she walked towards the bathroom door Raffa swung at her, punching her in the eye and then in her jaw. She fell back and feeling dizzy she struggled to get back up on her feet. "I told you not to pick up that phone!" He screamed.

She ran into the bathroom grabbed a towel and covered her eye. It did nothing to stop the pain. Taking the towel away from her eye and looking down at the bursts of bright red on the clean white towel, she almost fainted. Turning on the faucet she wet and wrung out another towel and held that over her eye.

Within seconds of climbing into the bathtub with the kids, Deasia heard the door bust open. The kids were clawing at her and crying loudly now. They were terrified. As hard as she tried she couldn't comfort them.

The police were shouting for her to come out with her hands up. "Don't move until I tell you to!" She ordered the kids. She turned the bathroom doorknob and dropping the bloody towel she walked out with her hands up.

Right away she noticed Raffa lying face down on the bed, his hands cuffed behind his back.

Two of the agents went into the bathroom as another agent grabbed her, turned her around and handcuffed her. The agent then pulled her over to the other bed. Another agent brought several more towels from the bathroom and placed one over Deasia's eye.

She could tell from the kids crying they were getting further away. "Where are they taking my babies," She screamed, "Bring me my kids!" The agent told her to calm down, your kids are safe. "What happened to your face?" She glared at Raffa as the agents pushed him towards the door. "I fell out of bed when you pounded on the door. I was scared."

An hour later she was sitting in an office with one arm handcuffed to a chair and one arm free so she could drink a coffee.

"You are being charged with kidnapping, a federal offense. You crossed state lines with children illegally in your custody. You may also be charged as an accomplice in every crime your boyfriend committed," We can talk about all that later for now do you have anyone here in Atlanta that can come pick up your children?"

Deasia sobbed. "I have a cousin here. She might pick them up and keep them until you let me out of here." It was a long shot. Deasia hadn't physically seen this cousin since they were 15 years old. They'd been in touch daily through Facebook.

"You may want to make more permanent arrangements. You won't be going anywhere, anytime soon."

Sobbing again she gave the agent the woman's phone number and then asked if he would call DJ "They're so scared they need their father." Hating that she even thought it, she needed him too.

~

DJ made his way up into the rafters, again and quickly crawled to a back corner to check on his little secret. Picking up a section of insulation he pulled out a backpack and brushed it off. He unzipped it and looked inside. His secret was safe. He zipped the bag up and put it back in its hiding place.

Hearing screaming outside he made his way to a location where he could look down and see the door.

Jimmy parked down the street watching as gang members tried the side door and then as they boosted a guy up to peer into a long narrow, barred window. He texted DJ *You up there.* DJ was startled by the text alert and almost dropped his phone into the showroom. *Yep. What's going on?* Jimmy answered, *Sit tight.*

For the second time geared up agents and law enforcement officers stormed the street outside Jimmy's shop. They worked quickly, rounding up the four gang members that had been trying to get into the warehouse.

Got them! After breathing a huge sigh of release DJ made his way down into the showroom as Jimmy opened the door and came inside. DJ ran to the door and went out onto the sidewalk and watched as officers were putting gang members into the backs of unmarked cars.

"Not so tough and mighty now are you? FUCK YOU!" He screamed. Jimmy grabbed him and ushered him back into the shop. "The neighbors are all out there DJ Stop screaming! Look at that," Jimmy said pointing to a pick-up truck with the letters ICE on the passenger door on the driver's side, "That's what your President is doing for you!" "Fuck you too Jimmy," DJ answered. "Fuck you too Donald!" Jimmy laughed.

Jimmy's phone rang. It was Frank. They spoke for a few minutes. He hung up and told DJ, "They got your kids, they're safe." "Where, where are they? Can I see them?" "Frank said Atlanta. He said he'd be by in a little bit to talk to you." Jimmy assured him.

Ezee showed up with coffee and handed DJ a check for $32,000. He almost fell over. "Thank you man," DJ said, "This lowers my stress level so much. My kids. My bills. Thank you both. I owe you guys my life." "What did you say?" Jimmy asked loudly. The three of them laughed. "Don't spend it yet DJ," Jimmy said, "You want to be smart and make sure it will last until you can get back to work."

"You know what they say about folks that save a life?" DJ asked. Jimmy and Ezee laughed. "That's right bitches you are responsible for that life, forever." DJ laughed.

Hours passed before Frank showed up. "I'm sorry. What a cluster fuck this day started out to be. It's all good now," He said, "But DJ you are going to need to testify at some point." DJ's stomach sank. "Against MS13? They'll kill me for sure." DJ answered. "Sorry man it's necessary. We'll do what we must do to keep you safe." "What about my kids are they okay? Can I go get them?" "Do you know Deasia's cousin, Maya?" "I know the name." "She picked the kids up and will take care of them until you can get there." "But I'm not allowed to leave the state, the judge said." "We'll make an exception," Frank said, "In this case you have primary custody. They can only leave Georgia with you." "What about Deasia," DJ asked, "Will they keep her there?" "She'll be extradited to New Jersey but that may take a while. She'll be in custody until then. I doubt they'll give her a chance to bail out. She's a flight risk."

DJ had mixed feelings about Deasia. Part of him delighted in the thought of her behind bars looking all pathetic and another part of him missed her and the life they had before drugs wreaked havoc on their family.

Jimmy took DJ to the bank to deposit the check and back at the shop Jimmy booked his flight from Atlantic City to Atlanta for first thing in the morning and a return flight for four people in the evening.

He was tempted to walk out of the shop and go buy a car, new clothes and to have a decent meal. Hearing Jimmy's voice in his head loud and clear he knew he couldn't do that. He had to be smart.

Frank texted him Maya's phone number and he immediately dialed the number. He thanked her for putting herself out there and rescuing his children. He told her he would arrive around two the next afternoon and he'd be going right back to the airport with the kids.

Then he spent the next half hour speaking to the kids he hadn't seen in so long. He could feel their excitement and it made him emotional. He couldn't stop his tears. When he told them, they'd be coming back home on a plane, they squealed with delight. "We hate long car trips," His son said, "They're so boring!"

DJ told them to be polite and good for Maya and he promised to see them the next day.

Ezee, Jimmy, Frank, Steve, and DJ went out to a bar to get dinner and to decompress after all the excitement. "What do you'll think?" DJ asked, "Do you think it's over or are these gang bangers never going to quit? I need to bring my kids home tomorrow to their house and I gotta tell you I'm a lot anxious about it." "We don't know for sure," Frank started, "But what I do know is if there's anyone here we haven't picked up, they're going to be running or at least crawling under a rock for a long time."

They stayed out too late, and DJ drank a bit too much. He set the alarm on his phone for 7:00 a.m.

Jimmy arrived at the shop, coffee, and breakfast sandwiches in hand. "How are you feeling?" He asked DJ "Besides the hangover I'm good. I feel safe for the first time in a long time and I'm so excited about seeing the kids. I can't tell you the sick feeling I've been dealing with. I've been so worried."

He did feel safer but there was still a little voice inside nagging and reminding him that he robbed terrorists and at any time they could come out of the woodwork and strike.

Feeling like a confident, seasoned traveler, he thanked Jimmy for the lift to the Atlantic City Airport and went through security without incident.

Hartsfield-Jackson Atlanta Airport was overwhelming, and DJ's confidence waned. He made his way onto the right train and found his way to the ride share waiting area.

Once he was in the back of the car, he texted Mayo to let her know he was on his way.

His phone rang startling him. He assumed it was Maya, but it was a recording asking him to accept charges for a call from Deasia. Without thinking, a habit he was desperately trying to break, he answered.

"I'm sorry." Deasia said. When DJ didn't answer she asked, "Did you pick up the kids?" "I'm on my way now." He answered. "You're in Atlanta?" Hesitantly DJ said, "Yes." "DJ I'm so sick. Will you bail me out? I need to go home, please DJ" She cried.

DJ froze. He had no idea how to react. Jimmy's words, "Think before you make a bad decision." Swirled through his mind. "I heard they refused you bail." "Can't you do something, I'm sorry for everything. I can't believe the horrible things I've done to you, to our babies. Please forgive me, please help me?" She pleaded.

DJ took a deep breath. He decided not to give a yes or no answer. As soon as he got home he'd ask Jimmy's advice. "I might consider helping you once you get to New Jersey and only if you agree to go straight into treatment, long term treatment." "Did you hear they were sending me to Jersey?" "Yep. That's what I heard. I got to go. Our kids are waiting on me. They've been through a lot, they're scared. That right there is a lot to forgive." He told her to think about what he said and told her she could call the following morning to speak with the kids.

Tears filled his eyes as the car rounded a corner and caught a glimpse of his kids, standing on the sidewalk. “James looks like he’s grown at least a foot.” He said to himself. From the distance Maya looked like Deasia. Not as much up close but there was a family resemblance. He was barely out of the car and the kids tackled him.

After speaking briefly with Maya, and expressing his gratitude for her help, he ordered a rideshare and piled the kids in the vehicle. They were off to the airport. During the forty-five-minute ride DJ couldn’t stop smiling and the kids couldn’t stop talking. They spoke a lot about swimming, restaurants, motels and having lots of fun. Then they told the story of the police coming into their hotel room early in the morning and explained to DJ how they had to hide in the bathroom. It was painful to see how scared and sad they were when they told him how they took their mom away and then took them to the police station.

His sadness was replaced with excitement as they approached the airport. Jasmine was looking forward to flying but told DJ she was a little bit scared.

They got something to eat, and DJ bought them each a drink and an etch a sketch to keep them busy during the flight.

When they landed in New Jersey DJ turned his phone back on. Deasia tried to call three times. He deleted the calls. There was no way he was going to let her suck him back into her nightmare.

Unsure of how he would feel once back in his home, DJ was grateful to have the kids there to distract him from dwelling on what happened there.

The kids were eerily calm. They quietly played with their favorite toys and walked around quietly getting reacquainted with their home.

Deasia called that night and told DJ she made the decision to go to rehab. Once she got back to New Jersey she would make a request to the court. She asked DJ if he would find a place. He allowed her to speak briefly with the kids.

Chapter 24:
One Year Later

No smoking on beach or boardwalk

Ezee, Jimmy and DJ sat on a boardwalk bench puffing away on Garcia Vega Elegante cigars, directly underneath the no smoking sign. DJ picked the cigars up in honor of his mentor, Levi. Over the past year, Levi coached DJ on business and financial success. DJ was finally starting to understand why the old man still drove a 1999 Cadillac. It was because there was nothing wrong with the car. It was a classic and worth more than it was when it he first purchased it.

DJ also spent hours over the last year being mentored by Jimmy on business and more importantly on thinking things through before making decisions. He stressed to his friend, if you aren't sure run the idea, no matter how big or small by someone else before making the wrong decision.

The three unlikely friends had been exploring mutual working possibilities over the last year.

One idea under consideration was politics. They imagined a Black man, a cop and a Hispanic man joining forces and running for city council as Republicans. They considered the votes they could deliver for each other and for the up ticket. "We would be a force to reckon with for sure." DJ smirked. "Consider this though," Jimmy started, "What if we hand- picked candidates and supported them behind the scenes financially and gathered votes for them?" Ezee added, "That way we could run our own business and be sure the people running our city have everyone's best interests at heart, especially ours!" They all laughed.

Save the Turtles

Next to the no smoking sign was a save the turtles, sign. "Who the hell puts these stupid signs up?" Ezee asked, "The turtles have survived for the past 2000, probably many more years without our help." Jimmy laughed. "Some bitch in Florida decided she didn't want cars driving on the beach in front of her house, so she came up with the idea to save the turtles. It caught on and she got her wish." "I got nothing against turtles," DJ said, "They're ugly and mean but I don't want them, or their eggs hurt. Who does?" "That's how she got away with it, who wants to be the person that says screw those turtles." Jimmy answered. "Somebody needs to veto all this shit." Ezee added.

The last year was rough for Jimmy. As a result of lifting the granite counter during the shootout at the shop, he reinjured his back. Surgery left him unable to work most of the year. With only Maria's salary, money was tight and getting tighter.

He passed the time by putting in a new kitchen for Maria and completing work on the income property across the street with heavy lifting help from Ezee. They finally found a nice family to rent that house which would hopefully help financially.

Looking forward to getting to work with his two new partners Jimmy knew the sooner the better.

Real estate investors thinking they would get steals on property because of the empty casinos were descending on the city in large numbers. Jimmy thought they could find properties for sale off the boardwalk and convince investors how much better those locations would be for them and their business.

Ezee and DJ weren't a hundred percent sold on Jimmy's idea. "What if some billionaire comes in here from China and wants to build a hotel in the middle of town and we find out all he wants to do is bring in illegal immigrants and launder money?" DJ questioned.

"It's a lot to think about but we need to make a decision pretty quick here." Ezee answered. "This is why we'll have the right politicians in place," Jimmy started, "It'll be their job to vet those people. We need to sell them the property get our cut and move on, hoping we've picked the right people to run the city."

"I gotta get going," Ezee said, "It's a big day and an even bigger night!"

As the three of them started to get up, Five F/A-18 fighter jets buzzed the boardwalk at seven hundred miles an hour, or Mach 1 which is the speed of sound.

"This patriotic stuff is terrifying sometimes!" DJ yelled as he jumped off the bench. Ezee and Jimmy fist pumped each other and laughed.

The jets were practicing for the Atlantic City Airshow that would be taking place later that afternoon.

Up and down the boardwalk venders were setting up their booths. This air show is one of the largest and most impressive in the country. There was so much to see in the air and all sorts of attractions to see on the ground as well.

Traditionally after the airshow Ezee threw one of his famous picnics and today would be no different. "You ready for tonight, Pyro?" Ezee asked. "You better believe it," DJ answered, "It's been a while, but I intend to impress. I got the music all synchronized up, ready to rock!"

Both of his ex-bosses agreed to take DJ back, so he was working at his security job and at the accountant's office again. Most of the neighborhood residents were happy he was also back to putting on out of this world fireworks displays.

He'd been so careful with the twenty-thousand dollars he secretly collected and stashed from the Brooklyn convenience store. It was so hard not to tell anyone, but especially difficult to keep it from Ezee and Jimmy. He felt awful about keeping the secret but every now and then he took a few hundred out and surprised Deasia and the kids with a little something special.

Keeping Deasia in treatment took all the *Go Fund Me* money. She spent six-months at a center in California. Back home now with DJ and the kids she was doing well, and still attending meetings daily. DJ was daring to think, just maybe they might be getting back together. Their divorce papers were never officially filed at the courthouse, so technically they were still married.

She surprised DJ by registering for college courses and telling him she wanted to be a drug and alcohol counselor.

Luckily the MS13 members that were arrested and charged with several counts of attempted murder and stalking DJ pleaded guilty so he didn't need to testify in court which would have set him up for retaliation.

Not much else came out of the terrorism case. Several agencies were still investigating and every now and then someone would stop by to try and jog DJ or Jimmy's memory with questions or photos.

Chapter 25:
The Notification

It turned out to be one of the best summer days any of them could remember. The airshow was more impressive than ever. There's something about the sight and sounds of the United States Air Force Thunderbirds and the United States Navy Blue Angels that leave you feeling proud of the country we call home.

That night with the beautiful bay as a backdrop and the aroma of hamburgers and hot dogs on the grill, the neighborhood felt almost normal again.

Fausta didn't always attend her son's picnics; it was nice to see her enjoying time with her daughter and grandchildren who were visiting from Puerto Rico. Benny was having a fun time.

Jimmy would be lying if he said he wasn't slightly on edge. He walked the perimeter of the park several times while keeping a close eye on Maria.

There were rumblings that MS13 was trying to reestablish themselves in the area. Deasia turned out to be a valuable informant for Frank. She remained friendly with DJ who occasionally let out bits and pieces of intel.

Most of the convenience stores in town had all new employees. Jimmy was keeping a close eye on activity in and around the stores. DJ never wanted to see another convenience store, ever. There are several coffee shops in Atlantic City, and he recently set out to give each of them a try, hoping one would be better than the rest. So far they were all good which was making his decision to pick a favorite difficult.

The bayfront park was full. Every neighbor showed up. As the sky turned from baby blue to a pinkish color you would have been able to hear a pin drop. All eyes were focused on the bay. Jimmy took a few steps back so he could take in the whole scene.

The water was still. Seagulls were perched on the top rail of a fence off to the right. A slight breeze came through as the sky exploded, exposing the brightest orange, red and pink colors. The sun, a huge ball of bold orange descended slowly into the horizon leaving behind darker shades of red and orange.

It was too perfect to be real.

Within seconds of the last bit of orange disappearing into the bay the music was turned up and the party was back on. Anticipation for the next show in the sky was building.

DJ did not disappoint. The fireworks were so fabulous that even Atlantic City's finest stood back and watched the entire show before telling DJ they had a complaint, only one.

The party went on well into the night. Everyone behaved and had an exciting time.

Jimmy stayed to help Ezee, and DJ clean up. They talked as they drug trash bags to the curb and the three of them finally agreed on a business. Determined to do whatever it took to turn the city around they were convinced Real Estate investing was the right business for them.

They decided to go out to breakfast to discuss the details and to celebrate.

~

Morning came entirely too soon. Jimmy decided to walk the few blocks to the diner. He was on his second cup of coffee when DJ and Ezee finally showed up.

They were deep into a discussion on the planning of their new business venture when DJ's phone played one line of Mo Money Mo Problems by Notorious B.I.G.

Ezee and Jimmy looked at him as he sat frozen. "What the hell is it?" Jimmy finally blurted out.

DJ looked at the notification and then handed his phone across the booth to Ezee, who was sitting next to Jimmy.

$50,000,000 has been deposited in an account in Alexandria, Egypt in your name.

"Boys I believe we may be going on our first business trip!" DJ said with a smirk as he passed his phone to Ezee, and then to Jimmy.

"No! NO, NO, NO we don't have enough building left for them to shoot up!" Jimmy said a bit too loud.

About The Author

David Tayoun is the son of a powerful Philadelphia politician, who also owned a Middle Eastern Restaurant that employed many immigrant employees.

He graduated from Julia R. Masterman High School in Philadelphia and received his bachelor's degree in Criminal Justice from Temple University. David attended Capitol Law School.

He started his career in the Philadelphia Municipal Courts working with Parolee's in the FOD (First Offender Drug Unit Program).

David went on to become a member of the Atlantic City Police Department and received the Officer of the Year award. He served in the special Investigations Section and on uniform patrol. He retired from the force due to injuries sustained when he was struck by a stolen car during a chase.

Involving himself in politics in Atlantic City he amassed a loyal voter base. David was appointed as Director of Neighborhood Services for the City of Atlantic City, which oversees all business licensing and regulations and all aspects of the construction industry.

After leaving public life David started a successful Kitchen Cabinet and Granite shop employing many local, residents in need of a second chance.

He currently heads a development group TBC Enterprises LLC and runs Tayoun's War House LLC.

About The Author

Early Reviews For STUNG

Started reading and had to finish but didn't want it to end. I could not put it down. The story seems like it was straight from news headlines, and it captured my interest with regards to greed and ID theft. If it were a movie with right cast, it would be riveting! Thomas Madamba ~ Atlantic City Police Captain, retired.

Unexpected twists throughout, I had to binge read! There better be a sequel. Nora Truscello~ Two-time best-selling author and international lecturer

I've always enjoyed a good thriller and this one is up there with the best. ~Captain James L. Andros, Atlantic City Police Captain, retired.

The characters were so well crafted! A great story of how three completely different men form a lifetime bond. This story has it all, action, adventure, family drama and a true sense of place. It was educational as well. Identity theft is happening everywhere! Doreen McGettigan~ Best-selling author, speaker, President of Intrepid Marketing

CPSIA information can be obtained
at www.ICGtesting.com
Printed in the USA
BVHW030644051122
651249BV00012B/273